Play Ball!

Play Ball!

CAROL MATAS

KEY PORTER BOOKS

For Michael Narhanson
Best son-in-law, dear friend, and baseball maven

National Library of Canada Cataloguing in Publication

Matas, Carol, 1949–
Play ball! / Carol Matas.

ISBN 1-55263-557-0

I. Title.

PS8576.A7994R67 2003 jC813'.54 C2003-906023-3

The publisher gratefully acknowledges the support of the Canada Council for the Arts and the Ontario Arts Council for its publishing program. We acknowledge the support of the Government of Ontario through the Ontario Media Development Corporation's Ontario Book Initiative.

We acknowledge the financial support of the Government of Canada through the Book Publishing Industry Development Program (BPIDP) for our publishing activities.

Key Porter Books Limited
70 The Esplanade
Toronto, Ontario
Canada M5E 1R2

www.keyporter.com

Electronic formatting: Jean Peters

Printed and bound in Canada

03 04 05 06 07 08 6 5 4 3 2 1

Chapter 1

"Rosie!"

"What?"

"Hurry up. We'll be late."

Abe stood at the kitchen door, lunch pail in hand, waiting for me. Joe stood beside him, his nose in a book, as usual.

"So?" I answered despondently.

"So," Mama answered for Abe, "you can't be late on your first day of school."

I rolled my eyes, and continued to sit at the kitchen table pretending to eat my porridge. What did Mama know? She was so busy doing her union work and managing the nickelodeon for Papa that she had barely noticed what a miserable time I'd had at school since we'd moved to Chicago in the winter. And over the summer I'd made no friends either. Me, who never had trouble making friends! And now here we were, our first day back to school after the holidays, and I was dreading it. Why?

Horrible Hannah! That's what I called her from the first moment I talked to her. It was my first day at my new school. I'd walked in happy, looking forward to making new friends. Right away I'd noticed that there were only five girls in the class, but I thought that would be a good thing because they'd be easier to get to know. But Hannah had put a stop to that.

"We have no more room in our group," she said to me.

"No more room?" I asked, puzzled.

"That's right," she confirmed. She turned her back on me in the school yard and marched the other girls away to skip rope, leaving me standing there all alone. I didn't give up though. I tried talking to the other girls when they were on their own, but they refused to talk back. Horrible Hannah had spoken. Papa said she was probably afraid I'd take over the group, and she had to be leader.

I sighed and pushed myself up from the table. There was one hope I could cling to, I told myself; next year I'd go to a new school for seventh grade, and things could get better. But today, a year sounded forever away.

It was still hot outside, so I didn't bother with a sweater. Mama had already braided my hair and then wound the braid up on the back of my head for a very grown-up look. Not that it mattered. I sighed again.

"I have a story for you," Mama began.

"Mama, we'll be late!" Abe objected.

"It's short," she answered. "There was a young student in New York. He was looking for Columbia University but he kept getting different directions, and he got lost. Finally, he spotted a professional-looking elderly man carrying a pile of books."

"Excuse me, sir," he said, "how do you get to Columbia University?"

The old man thought for a moment, then answered, "Study, young man. Study hard!"

She laughed.

"I know Mama," I said. "I get the point."

"Rosie, take your lunch pail," Mama reminded me. I picked it up and followed Abe and Joe out the door. We walked down one flight of stairs and then were out on Maxwell Street. When we first arrived in Chicago I thought we were right back where we used to live, on Orchard Street in New York. Maxwell Street was packed with people, either selling or buying. If you didn't want to buy from a pushcart, there were plenty of shops all along the street, which would no doubt have what you wanted.

Abe chattered to me over the shouting of the pushcart owners. "Fresh fish! Fresh chickens! Fresh . . ."

"So, tonight we play the Golems," Abe said. "Last time they beat us and they crowed over it, but tonight Johnny Cohen is back from visiting his relatives in New York and we'll flatten them like a piece of matzo."

Joe, who is just eight but always sounds older than his years, said, "They have a better pitcher, a better back catcher, *and* a better outfield."

Abe's face turned red. "Johnny Cohen is the best outfielder and hitter in this entire town. He'll make the difference, you'll see. And you think their back catcher is better than *me*? Your own brother?"

Joe shrugged.

Abe's eyes narrowed. "That's not very nice."

Joe shrugged again. "But true."

Abe kicked a stone. "I'm getting better."

"Of course you are," I said to him, glaring at Joe. He was honest to a fault.

"I need a better glove," Abe said defensively.

I tried to pay attention as my brothers continued talking baseball, but my stomach was in such a knot I could barely listen. We slowly made our way though the crowds. As soon as we turned onto Johnson, the din quieted a bit, but the noise was replaced by the shouts and laughter of children hurrying to our school, Garfield Elementary.

We arrived just as the teacher began ringing the bell. The girls and boys lined up separately to file in. Once we entered, a teacher stopped each of us and directed us to our new rooms. I had a tiny spark of hope that a new girl would be in class today—someone who would be friends with me.

Of course the first person I saw when I walked in was Horrible Hannah. She was sitting in the front row with Pearl, Jenny, Sarah, and Goldie. I scanned the room. No new girls. I sighed for the thousandth time that morning and made my way to the back, as far away from Horrible Hannah as I could get. As the tallest person in the room, including all the boys but one, the teacher would probably feel I was better off at the back anyway; the shorter students couldn't see unless they sat in front.

Mrs. McBride stood at the door and welcomed each student. It was rumored that she was very strict, with no sense of humor at all. She certainly looked fearsome, with a plain face, square jaw, thin lips, and gray hair pulled back in a bun. She didn't smile once. I squeezed myself into my desk, my knees touching the top, and stifled one more sigh.

Torture.

I arrived at the nickelodeon that evening just as Mrs. Nettle was leaving. She managed the nickelodeon closest to our house, and had to take a break every night to fix supper for her family. That's one reason why Papa had me working there. Abe was at the one a little farther down the street. We worked as ushers. I hurried into the small dressing room off the stage, changed into my uniform, tucked my hair into my hat, and hurried out to the front of the house.

I loved my usher's suit. I wore a long-sleeved white shirt, knickers that buckled just over the knees, and criss-crossed gray-and-black stockings. My cap was also a soft gray. Papa had dressed me as a boy—and I loved playing the part. Because I was so tall, no one could tell I was a girl unless I spoke. And after a few weeks of play-acting a boy's voice, I had everyone completely fooled. I would swagger up and down the aisles showing people to their seats, sell apples, peanuts, and ice-cream sticks, scold the rowdies—and they would listen!

This was the main reason why I had made no friends on our street—my job at the nickelodeon. During the summer I worked all day, and sometimes into the night.

"What's on today, Papa?" I asked as we met up in the lobby.

"Oh, it's one of your favorites," Papa answered. "It's a Western."

After I had everyone settled and the movie began I saw it was the one called *The Cattle Rustlers.* It had been made by a company right here in Chicago. They had sent their actors out west to make the film. Every time I watched it I felt a yearning inside that I couldn't explain. The country looked so wild and free, the skies like they went on forever. The cowboys rode their horses at a gallop—a speed that seemed both terrifying and exhilarating. Secretly, deep down inside, I wondered if one day I could be a cowboy, or rather, a cowgirl like Annie Oakley from the Wild West Show.

In *The Cattle Rustlers,* a production assistant accidentally moved into one of the shots, and the company left the mistake in. Papa said they did it because it's too expensive to reshoot. I didn't mind, I still loved the story. First the bad guys stole cattle from the good guys—it's called cattle rustling. Then they branded the cattle with their own brand. The good guys chased the bad guys and there was a fierce shoot-out with gun smoke everywhere. The villain was shot. He went to a cabin to recover, but the hero tracked him there, and they had a final fight. Then the villain was defeated and hanged, but we didn't see the hanging. When it was over, Papa, as he did on every break, took center stage and sang songs to entertain the audience until the reel was changed. And then the next story started.

Unlike at school, time always flew by when I was in the theater. Before I knew it Mrs. Nettle was back, and it was time for me to go home for dinner. I had to fix it because Mama went to her union meetings straight from the nickelodeon down the street. I couldn't believe it, but no sooner had we arrived in Chicago than she was helping to organize a garment workers' strike just like she had in New York!

Abe came and picked me up at the door.

"Hurry!" he said. "My game is in half an hour."

"So late?" I asked. It was almost seven.

"It'll be light for ages. We're playing in the empty lot on Oak Street."

And so we made our way home though the crowds. Joe was already there when we arrived, ensconced in a chair, deep into a book. It was *The Prince and the Pauper* by Mark Twain.

I put out some cold smoked meat, boiled potatoes, beets, pickles, and a large loaf of pumpernickel bread. We ate quickly, in silence; we were too hungry to talk. As soon as Abe finished he rushed off, leaving Joe and me on our own. I washed up the dishes, then began to prepare the meal for tomorrow. I cleaned the potatoes and put them on the stove to boil. Mama had left a chicken, and I put that on to boil as well with some carrots and parsnips. It would all keep in the icebox until tomorrow; Joe had made sure the iceman had left us a large new block of ice.

The evening was cool; a wonderful relief from the heat and humid weather of the summer. Although it was September, Papa said we could probably expect a few more weeks of warm weather and then an earlier winter than we had had in New York.

As the food cooled I put out the ironing board and began to prepare everyone's clothes for the next day. Joe read aloud to me from his book. What a wonderful story it was. A prince changing places with a pauper. A pauper pretending to be a prince!

Suddenly Abe burst into the kitchen and threw his glove on the floor.

"Johnny has gone and broken his leg!"

"No!" I exclaimed.

"Yes. He slid right into that brute Larry Steinfield on first base. Larry blocked him in this way that was bound to cause trouble!"

"What way?" I asked.

"Oh, I don't know," Abe groaned. "He just wouldn't move."

"Well, that doesn't sound so evil," I remarked.

"That's not the point!" Abe exclaimed. "Johnny was our best player. And you know how those German Jews from the South Side look down on us. We have one more game with them on Sunday. We have to win this last one of the season. Otherwise we'll have to hang our heads all winter whenever we see them!" He paused and thought for a moment. "We need a ringer."

"Ask Rosie," Joe said calmly.

Abe smacked his hand on the table. "This is no time for jokes. We're in trouble."

"Ask Rosie," Joe repeated. "She's a better player than any you've got."

"But she's a girl!" Abe scoffed.

"Not when she's dressed like a boy," Joe offered.

Abe stood still, looking thunderstuck.

I took no notice. It was a crazy idea.

"It could work," Abe said slowly.

I laughed. "No, it wouldn't. Someone would recognize me. Someone from school. They'd know I'm a girl."

"There are only a couple of boys from our school on our team," Abe said. "And they're not in your class. They'd never catch on."

I bit my lip as I considered the idea seriously for the first time. Abe knew I loved to play baseball. "Do you really think I could do it?"

"*I* do," Joe said.

"So do I," Abe agreed, a smile spreading across his face. "And you even have the clothes."

"My usher's clothes," I said, grinning. "It would be . . . daring, wouldn't it?"

"It would," the boys said together.

"We'll have to ask Papa," I cautioned them. "He'd have to spare us from the nickelodeons. And you know Sunday is his busiest day."

"You leave Papa to me," Abe said. "I'll convince him." He paused. "Does that mean you'll do it?"

"I will," I declared. "I'll do it!"

Chapter 2

My heart thudded in my chest. This was our big moment. Would the plan work? I stood beside Abe, cracking gum, trying to look cool as a cucumber. Johnny's mitt was tucked under my arm. Mr. Kobrinsky, the coach, stood rocking back and forth, heel to toe, as if he were praying. He wore a long jacket and a cap on his head. He had blue eyes, a big black beard, a mustache, and a stocky build, like a wrestler.

"So, *nu,*" he said to me, "you're a cousin to Abe?"

I nodded.

"Name?"

Name? I hadn't even thought of one. Rosie . . .

"Roy," I answered, trying to keep my voice low.

"Royter? The red one? Got a temper then?" he asked, with a hint of a smile.

I shrugged. My papa's name was Roy, which was why I thought of it. And he *had* been called that because he had had such a temper when he was a baby that his face would turn red. But he always seemed calm now no matter what happened. He also had red hair, and so did I.

"Welcome, Roy," he said. "You'll play right field, and bat third. And remember, 'The race is not to the swift, nor the battle to the strong.'" He paused. "Do you know where those words are from?"

I shook my head.

"Ecclesiastes."

"But it doesn't make sense—not for baseball," I objected. "Swift and strong *do* win in baseball."

"Ah, an argument you'll give me?"

"Yes." I grinned. I loved to argue.

"Good, good," he said with a small smile. "It's the Jewish way, to argue. Our forefathers argued with God all the time. And as for your comment that the swift and strong will win, it looks that way on the surface, perhaps. But the surface isn't what's real."

"It isn't?"

"No. There are many layers beneath the surface. They

are what is real." He paused again. "Do you think you are simply what I see?"

Well, I knew I wasn't because I was in disguise. But normally I was. Wasn't I?

"I'm not sure," I answered.

"If you aren't sure, then there might be more than meets the eye, no?"

"Maybe."

"In all things that's true," he said.

Abe pulled at my arm. "I better take him to meet the others," he said.

Mr. Kobrinsky nodded and gave me a small wink.

As we walked away Abe whispered, "They say he studies cabala and the mysteries of the universe."

"And he's a baseball coach?" I asked.

"He says baseball is a good mirror for life. A perfect metaphor. Whatever that means."

"It means," I said, proud of my knowledge, "that it represents something—in this case, life."

Abe stopped near the first-base line. "You don't think he suspected you, do you?"

"He would have said something, I'm sure," I said with a smile. "So far, so good."

As we talked I looked around and examined my surroundings. We had taken a streetcar to the South Side, and then walked to a park beside one of the schools. The richer Jews lived here on tree-lined streets in two- or three-story brick houses. The school was modern and large, the park next to it filled with trees.

It wasn't only the surroundings that were impressive. On the third-base side the Tigers' fans had gathered. The women wore fancy dresses and hats and held parasols over their heads. The men were dressed in three-piece suits and cloth hats.

On the first-base side the Chavarims' fans had congregated. The women wore long black dresses or skirts and shirtwaists, with tiny hats or even *babushkas.* The men wore jackets and caps. The Tigers' fans had brought folding chairs; ours had brought blankets to sit on.

Papa said we could afford to move to the South Side now, but with all four of his nickelodeons on Maxwell Street, he needed to be near the businesses. Besides, Mama wanted to be near the striking workers. I didn't mind Maxwell Street. It reminded me of home.

The Tigers ("the Golems" was just what Abe and his friends called them) were looking smart in their uniforms: cream-colored shirts and black knickers. They even wore special shoes. And their caps had large T's sewn on the front.

Abe saw me looking around. "Pretty fancy, huh? They're almost all German Jews living here. And what snobs! They think we Russians are peasants. Lowest of the low. Just wait. You'll see. That's why we *need* to beat them. One last game. Teach them a lesson."

Some of the Tigers began to call to our team: "Why don't you just go home! Give up now!"

The Chavarim called back, "Golems! Golems go home!"

"This happens every game," Abe said dismissively as the catcalls went back and forth.

"Why does your team hate the German Jews so much?" I asked Abe. "Don't they arrange these games?"

"They do," he admitted. "But only to make us look bad," he grumbled.

"I doubt that's why the adults do it," I contradicted him. "They probably want to bring the Jewish community together."

Suddenly Abe clutched my arm. "Is that Papa?" He pointed to just beyond first base, a little way past where the adults had gathered. It *was* Papa. And he was setting up a camera on a tripod!

"Since when does he have a camera?" I asked Abe.

Abe shrugged. He smiled and waved. We hurried over to him.

"Isn't she a beauty?" Papa grinned and gestured toward the camera.

"Amazing," I said.

"She's an Edison," he said proudly. "I'm going to film the game as my first project!" He laughed. "Don't worry, it will be practice for me; I won't be showing it to anyone."

Soon everyone had gathered round to see the machine. It was a good opportunity for Abe to introduce me to my new teammates. Members of the other team trickled over for a look too. Papa had been talking a lot lately about making a film, but I hadn't really been paying attention. He said he didn't like the ones offered and would probably do better himself. "I'll hire actors," he'd said, "and we'll do Shakespeare and Ibsen. Make movies that'll bring culture to the people!"

A baseball game is hardly culture, I thought, *but I guess he has to start somewhere.*

Meanwhile, out on the field the coaches were shaking hands. The two umpires were taking their places, one behind home plate, another behind second base. The Tigers had home field advantage, which meant we batted first.

Our bench was on the first-base side; the Tigers had a bench on the third-base side. Abe and I sat down together. A fellow called Izzy sat down beside me. He was short and thin, but looked like he might be my age, twelve, rather than Abe's, just eleven. Some of the boys looked as old as thirteen. Izzy had *payas,* which showed he was very

Orthodox, maybe from a Hasidic family. I could also see *tsitsis* dangling from beneath his shirt.

"*Nu,*" he said, "you're Abe's cousin? Where are you from?" He spoke in Yiddish but I understood. I had refused to speak anything but English since I was five years old, but both Papa and Mama spoke Yiddish at home.

Where *was* I from? I hadn't thought to create a whole history for my new self.

"New York," I answered, thinking that wasn't entirely a lie. I *was* from New York. I made sure to keep my voice low, which came naturally after so much practice at the nickelodeon.

"Are you here for long?"

"My mother is ill," I replied, thinking back to Mama's illness of last year. She had almost died. "And my father is looking after her, so here I am. I could go home at any time," I added.

"'As long as a person breathes, he should not lose hope.'" Izzy nodded. And he added, "That's a quote from the Talmud."

"Hmm," I said, as if I had an idea what he was talking about. Was Talmud the same as Torah? I dared not ask, in case he thought I was ignorant. Which I was, in fact, of all religious matters. Mama didn't believe in any of it, and I had no religious training at all.

The first batter stepped up to the plate.

"That's Joe," Abe said. "We call him Crazy Joe."

"Why?" I asked.

"He has his own style of playing," Izzy said. "You'll see. He plays the outfield with us. He's in left, I'm center, you're in right."

Joe was tall and skinny. He wore a cap and a rather dirty shirt.

"It looks like he's already been sliding into home plate," I remarked.

"He probably has," Abe grinned. "He lives for baseball."

The Tigers' pitcher was a plump boy with a surprisingly good arm. He struck Joe out in three pitches. The Tigers hooted after Joe as he walked off the field. But worse than that, the pitcher tipped his hat at Joe as he departed, an action that seemed sarcastic and taunting.

"Who's the pitcher?" I asked.

"His name is Morley," Abe answered. "He loves to rub it in when he strikes someone out. That's Max," Abe said, as the next boy walked to the batter's box. He plays shortstop." Max was rather pudgy for a shortstop.

"Don't be fooled," Abe said as he saw me eyeing him. "He's one of the fastest runners we have. Stealing, he's seven for ten."

I watched closely, trying to get an idea of what the

pitcher, Morley, might throw me. Butterflies were suddenly living in my stomach. Not only did I have to worry about being discovered, now I was worried about making a fool of myself. Abe could sense my unease.

"You're the best," he said. "Don't worry. Enjoy!"

He was right. This was a chance I might not get again. A real game. With players as good as me. Why worry? Why not enjoy?

The first pitch was a ball, which Max took. Next he fouled off a pretty good strike. Morley glared at Max, obviously trying to intimidate him, but Max glared right back. The next pitch came inside, and Max leaped back without saying a word. Our bench erupted in catcalls. On the next pitch Max hit a grounder right up the middle and in no time was on first. Abe was right. He *was* fast.

I was up next. I picked up the bat Max had dropped at the plate, and swung it to get the feel for the wood. Usually when I played with the boys I hit with a stick, not a real baseball bat. This was far heavier than I was used to. Being tall and strong, though, I knew I could turn around on the ball quickly if I saw a good pitch. I dug my foot into the dirt and stared out at the pitcher. He threw. I could see it perfectly; it was if it were moving in slow motion. I shifted my weight, and swung as hard as I could.

Thwack! The ball hit on the sweet spot of the bat and it carried and carried as I ran toward first. It was still in the air as I rounded second. I saw the coach waving to me to keep going, so I ran to third. The coach kept waving. I ran as fast as I could. Just before I reached home plate I heard the umpire yell, "Home run!"

My teammates leaped off the bench and ran over to me and Max. Had they known me better they probably would have mobbed me; as it was, though, I got handshakes all round. That was a good thing because although my hat was stuck on with at least ten pins it certainly could have been pulled off if they'd jumped all over me.

After accepting all the congratulations and *mazel tovs,* I sat back down on the bench beside Abe. "Told you," Abe grinned as he nudged me in the side. I grinned back.

I looked to see Papa waving. He'd caught it on film. I waved back. Impulsively I got up and hurried over to him.

"Good hit!" Papa said as soon as I reached his side.

"It was, wasn't it?" I grinned happily.

The next batter up was the second baseman, who had been introduced to me as David. He was nice looking and didn't wear a cap. He looked more like the Tigers' players, few of whom were Orthodox.

As I turned back toward Papa, I noticed that he was looking around nervously.

"What's the matter?" I asked him as I watched David foul-off two balls in a row.

"It's complicated," Papa answered.

David took two balls.

"What is?"

"It's the camera," Papa started to explain.

David took another ball and had a full count.

"What?" I asked, curious now.

"You should get back to the bench," Papa answered. "I'll tell you later, if I have to."

David swung through a pitch and went down. Morley tipped his hat again.

"All right," I said, feeling I should get back, but wondering what all the mystery was about.

Izzy was up to bat next, but by the time I'd returned to the bench he'd grounded out to short. The top of the inning was over, and we were up two to nothing. I picked up my mitt and headed out to right field.

I couldn't get over the beauty of the field we were playing on. There was real grass between the bases and even out in center field. I'd only played on a dirt field at school, or in an alley near our apartment in New York. I wondered if I'd be able to judge how fast I needed to run to get to the ball, and how differently it would bounce on grass.

A chalk line had been drawn on the grass to indicate

the boundaries of the baseball diamond. The ball I'd hit had landed dead center, just over the line. I adjusted my mitt, crouched a little, and waited.

Our pitcher, Lew, was tall and skinny. He quickly readied himself and threw his first pitch. It sailed over the head of the batter, a tough-looking customer.

"Hey!" the batter shouted.

Lew shrugged. Abe retrieved the ball and tossed it back. I could see him say something to the batter who quickly turned on Abe in a menacing way. My brother had always been sassy, but I could see he might be about to get into big trouble because of it. After a moment Abe crouched and pretended to ignore the guy. The batter seemed to think better of starting a fight and stepped back into the box.

Lew let loose again, this time with a strike that zoomed over the plate. Our bench cheered. But on the next pitch their batter connected with the ball and hit it far into left field. Crazy Joe started screaming, *"Bobkes! Bubkes!"* By screaming "it's nothing" at the top of his lungs, I figured he was trying to trick the runner into thinking he was going to make the catch, easily. He had a huge voice and I could see he *was* rattling the runner, who was slowing down after rounding first. Just as it seemed hopeless, Joe threw himself headfirst at the ball, slid in the grass, stuck his mitt out, and came up clutching the ball. I couldn't believe it! He casually threw it in to Lew as if it were a play he made every day.

Joe's shirt was now covered with grass stains, and it seemed that the dirtier he got the happier he was. I liked him. And I was beginning to see why he was called Crazy Joe.

Before I knew it Lew had struck out the next two batters. We headed back to the bench.

And that's when things started to get really complicated.

CHAPTER 3

"Izzy, Izzy! Over here!"

I turned to look. That voice. That voice was all too familiar.

Horrible Hannah! She was standing with the group of spectators, waving at Izzy.

"My sister," he said to me, waving back.

"Oh," I muttered. My heart sank, and I broke out into a sweat. She would show no mercy if she discovered who I was. This was a disaster! And I had to continue to sit next to Izzy. Because I'd gotten a hit, I couldn't suddenly change where I was sitting on the bench—if I did that, the other boys on the team would think I didn't know how things worked. I had to stay put.

Izzy certainly seemed much nicer than his sister. Now that I saw the way he was dressed, though, I was surprised that his sister attended school. I had thought very Orthodox girls didn't go to school, but stayed at home cooking and cleaning. That's what Mama always told me. That's one of the reasons she thought religion was bad for girls. "They're all like slaves," she'd say. Hannah, however, hardly behaved like a slave—more like a master!

Our first baseman, Aaron, was up to bat. I watched closely and tried not to think about Horrible Hannah. As Aaron took ball one, Coach Kobrinsky sauntered over.

"That was a nice swing," he said to me.

I didn't think he expected a reply, so I didn't make one.

"You like to study?"

I wasn't sure whether I'd heard him correctly. "Excuse me?"

"You like to study, Roy?"

"Uh, yes. I like school." I paused. "I like baseball better, though."

"Maybe you aren't looking at school the right way, then. You should look at it as if it *were* baseball. Figure out the questions you need to ask, the strategy of each book, the configuration of each math problem. . . ."

As we talked we both watched Aaron. He had two balls and two strikes, both foul-offs.

"Take Aaron, right now, for instance," Coach Kobrinsky said. "You could say the count is two and two and be done with it. Simple, no?"

I nodded.

"But there's more to those strikes then it seems. Both times he made good contact and just fouled the ball off. So I think that this time, he's going to get a hit."

Just then Aaron hit the ball hard into left field. He looked too thin for a hit like that! He took off like a startled animal, and pulled into second a good moment or two before the ball.

The coach shouted to the rest of the boys on the bench, "'Who ever persists in knocking will succeed in entering!'"

"Yes, Coach!" they all yelled back.

I looked at Abe and raised my eyebrows. Was this normal?

He shrugged and made a face that said I should get used to it.

Morris moved slowly to the batter's box. He looked like a really tough fellow. He had a big broad face with thick eyebrows, thick lips set in a prominent frown, a torn jacket, and ripped pants. He played third base.

"So what would you do if you were me, Roy?" asked Coach Kobrinsky. "Tell him to bunt or let him swing?"

"Well," I said, having no idea why he was asking me, "I'd have to know more before I could say." As we spoke Coach Kobrinsky pulled on his cap and made a signs with his hands.

"You'd have to know if he *can* bunt," the coach agreed.

"Or if he can hit," I added.

The coach smiled. "Good point."

"What do I do if I'm in that situation?" I added. "I don't know your signs."

"Better learn," the coach said, walking away.

Just then Morris swung and hit the ball foul.

"Morris isn't the bunting type," Abe said to me. "He thinks bunting is for sissies."

"I don't think bunting is very sensible," I remarked. "Why give the other team an extra out?"

As I watched Morris swing through two more balls, though, I supposed a bunt would have at least advanced the runner to third.

"Who's your new friend?"

That voice again. Hannah was standing behind us!

"This is Roy, Hannah," Izzy said. "Now go away. We're busy."

"Papa lets me stand here if I want," she objected.

"I thought Orthodox girls aren't allowed to talk to boys," I whispered to Abe.

Izzy overheard. "Girls and boys can't meet alone," he said. "But unfortunately, sisters don't count."

I was beginning to like Izzy—even though he had such a dreadful sister.

As Morris walked back to the bench, glowering, Abe got up. He was up to bat.

"Keep your shoulder tucked in," I warned him.

Morris glared at me as if it were my fault he'd just struck out. "Hey, listen to the *yannigan* giving advice!" he said. I knew very well that *yannigan* meant "rookie"—if you were being nice. If you weren't, it meant "second stringer."

"Lay off, Meshevsky," Izzy retorted. "Roy here didn't strike out. You did!"

Morris kicked the bench.

Coach Kobrinsky walked over. "'The patient in spirit is better than the proud in spirit.'" He patted Morris on the shoulder.

I expected Morris to shrug off his touch, but instead he almost grinned.

"That's better," Coach Kobrinsky said. "If we can't smile at ourselves, others will do it for us, won't they?"

Abe was a good hitter. Not as good as me, but solid. He had quick hands and could turn on a ball faster than most. He watched strike one go by. I wanted to shout my encouragement the way the other boys were, but with Hannah so close, I was afraid she'd recognize my voice. I noticed that before each pitch Abe touched his pants pocket. I knew he kept a lucky stone in there. It was a small reddish orange stone from Russia. Papa had given it to him for luck. He would no more have gone to a game without it than he'd go without his pants.

The next ball came in high, and Abe laid off it.

"You look familiar," Hannah said. She was standing far too close for comfort.

"Me?" I said, keeping my voice as low as possible.

"Yes, you. Where are you from?"

"New York."

"Well," she said, "keep up the good hitting. Those Jews we're playing against . . . I don't even know how they can call themselves Jews. You can smell the bacon all the way over here; they bring it in for their picnics. Look at the way they dress, too. Girls with short skirts, and short sleeves! No idea about modesty." She paused. "What do you think of them?"

I shrugged. I certainly didn't want to get into a conversation with her.

Abe laid off another ball.

"'Nothing reduces misfortune like patience!'" shouted the coach.

Abe hit the next ball. Foul.

Hannah continued. "They don't go to shul, half of them."

"Some of them might," I objected. She was starting to really get under my skin. Why did she think she was so much better than them? And wasn't that what everyone on this team hated about the other team, that they were stuck up and thought they were better than the Russian Jews?

Abe hit the next pitch sharply between first and second. The Tigers' first baseman dove for it, but the ball went just under his mitt. Abe made it safely to first and Aaron stopped at third. Now we had one out, with runners at first and third.

Our pitcher, Lew, was next up to bat. His blond hair stuck out of his cap. His face was covered with freckles that stood out against his fair skin. A wind picked up suddenly, and he had to settle his cap on his head more firmly. On the first pitch, he hit a line drive straight to the shortstop, who caught it on the fly, then threw the ball to first. A double play, and suddenly we were out of the top of the inning with nothing to show for it.

In a way I was relieved—I could now get away from Hannah. I put on my mitt and ran out into the field.

Lew quickly got ready. The Tigers' first baseman was up to bat. He was twice the size of the rest of us. He must have been almost six feet tall! He looked like he was twenty, not twelve or thirteen. He had an air about him, as if he knew no fear and was thinking about one thing, and one thing alone: smacking that ball. As Lew threw the first pitch, I instinctively backed up. I had just placed myself near the line when the batter tipped the pitch with the end of his bat. I could see it was not going to carry far, but would instead drop well in front of me. I sprinted forward, but the ball bounced, then died in the grass. I scooped it up and threw to first, but not in time to catch the runner.

"Way to go Larry!" I could hear coming from their bench. And to me, "Go home, *yannigan*!" And, "Go help your mama in the kitchen. Bake some strudel!" If they knew how close they were to the truth with those taunts!

My cheeks burned. I should've had that ball. But Lew was already pitching to the next batter, so I had to forget about the last play and concentrate on this one. One thing I did know: If I couldn't do that I'd be of no use to my team.

The next batter, the Tigers' right fielder, laid down a bunt on the first pitch. Abe grabbed it up as it dribbled toward the pitcher's mound, and threw to first for the out. It was his only choice. Their runner advanced to second.

I had to say that I was impressed with both teams. Everyone was playing very sound baseball; so far no one had made any serious mistakes. I decided not to be hard on myself about my last play. The ball could as easily have been hit right to me and I'd be a hero now. It wasn't so much a mistake or error as a bad guess.

The next batter hit a ball to Max, who bobbled it and threw to first—but not in time. Larry advanced to third, so the Tigers now had runners at first and third with only one out. Not good. The next batter hit a sharp grounder to third. Morris was able to hold the runner at third, so he chose to hang on rather than throw to first.

Bases loaded, one out.

Morley, the other team's pitcher, was up next. He swung his bat back and forth in preparation. Lew took a deep breath, then let loose. Morley smacked the ball, and I knew in an instant that it was coming right to me. I had to run for it, as fast as I could. I caught it on a bounce, and threw it to Abe, hard. He caught the ball and blocked the plate, but the runner, three times Abe's size, barreled into him and jolted the ball out of Abe's glove. The other team scored their first run—and the bases were still loaded.

Even though I'd made a play that could have been better and things didn't look good for our team, I couldn't help but feel happy just to be out on the field, to be playing a real game, and to be taken seriously as a player. I glanced at Papa and saw him filming. I could hardly wait to watch the film of this game!

The next batter, the Tigers' catcher, popped up behind the plate. Abe caught it. Two outs. The left fielder came up next. I guess he was trying too hard, because he swung wildly at pitches that weren't very good and struck out. *Could have been far worse,* I thought as I trotted off the field, remembering not to touch the lines. I didn't want to jinx myself!

Unfortunately, Hannah was still there, waiting for us as we took our seats on the bench.

"Nice throw," she commented. "You're very good, Roy."

I nodded my thanks.

"You might not want to get on the bad side of Larry, the Tigers' first baseman," she continued. "I've heard he waits for boys who rob him of a hit, then hurts them. He hurts them in horrible ways. Izzy, didn't Larry break Marty's arm?"

"Hannah, I'm sure Roy doesn't need to hear this," Izzy said.

"No, he doesn't," Abe agreed.

"Is it true?" I asked Abe.

"Afraid so," he said.

I looked over to first. Sure enough, Larry was glaring at me. He made a motion of his hand slitting his throat. Then he grinned at me.

"But I didn't even get him out," I said, confused.

"You *almost* did. You would have if Abe had held on to the ball," Hannah replied. "That's enough for Larry."

My heart sank. It was only the top of the third, and already I had an enemy. That couldn't be good.

Chapter 4

Crazy Joe was up to bat again. He started to call to the pitcher.

"Fun loiter hofenung ver ich noch meshugeh." Joe laughed, and so did the rest of the team. Everyone on our team knew he'd said, "Stuff yourself with hope, and you can go crazy!"

The pitcher just looked confused, mad, and frustrated—he obviously didn't speak Yiddish. "Ignorant greenhorns!" he called back.

Abe snorted. "They all think that speaking Yiddish is ignorant," he said.

Crazy Joe called back in Yiddish, "If the shoe fits, wear it!"

At this point the umpire stepped in. "Play ball! Play ball!" he called.

Crazy Joe pointed the bat at the pitcher for a moment in a menacing fashion.

"Hey, Morley," one of the Tigers called out, "don't let the moron bother you. You show him!"

Crazy Joe shouted, "Golems!" as he took a batting stance.

The rest of our bench picked up the chant, "Golems! Golems! Golems!"

This was fun! I joined in right away.

Morley, their pitcher, threw his pitch. It landed right in the dirt. It looked to me like Crazy Joe was having some kind of an effect on him. The second pitch was high and their catcher had to run to retrieve it. The third pitch was far outside. All this time our bench kept chanting, "Golems, Golems!"

The fourth pitch was high as well, and Crazy Joe took a walk to first base. Once there, I could see him say something to Larry. Larry went red. Crazy Joe laughed, darted off the bag, then back again. He was obviously thinking about stealing.

Max was up. He looked at Coach Kobrinsky, who was standing on the third-base line near the other team's bench. The coach was using signs. First he touched his cap, then his nose, then his ear, then his eye. Then he touched his cap again.

"You'd better teach me what those signs mean," I said to Abe, suddenly panicking. "What if I have to follow them?"

"First," Abe said, "remember that if he touches his cap twice you only follow the signs after he touches his cap the second time."

Max let the first pitch go by. Joe sprinted off the bag and then back, deciding not to steal—or maybe told not to steal by the coach.

"The sign to steal is Coach touching his ear," Abe said. "But only if you see it after the second time he touches his cap."

I saw the coach touch his cap again, then ear, nose, eye, nose, cap, and finally his nose.

"That's the signal for a hit and run," Abe whispered. "Nose means—" He was interrupted by Max smacking the ball and taking off. The ball went right to first base. but because Joe had left the bag early, he made it safely to second. Larry, thinking it would be an easy play, almost missed Max, he was so fast! But he did manage to tag Max out.

So now there was a runner on second, and I was up to bat again. I looked at the coach, but he wasn't giving any signs, so I supposed that meant I could swing away. As I moved into the batter box I heard Horrible Hannah yell, "Hit another homer, Roy!"

I just wanted a solid hit. With Joe's speed, I figured I could get him home that way. The other team started to razz me. *"Yannigan, Yannigan,"* they shouted. I tried to shut them out and concentrate. First pitch I fouled off. The second pitch I let go, but it was called a strike. I thought it was too high, but I wasn't about to argue with the umpire. I couldn't afford to call attention to myself in that way.

The next pitch was high too, but I swung for it and connected. The ball carried into right field and dropped just in front of the right fielder. I sprinted to first and got there just before the ball. Larry tagged me so hard I fell over into the dirt. He laughed. So did the rest of his team.

I got up, brushed myself off, and said, "I just pushed over another run. Think that's funny, blockhead?"

He growled like some sort of angry animal. Up close he looked even worse than from a distance. His eyes narrowed and he bared his teeth. Was he snarling?

"Next time you get a hit," he said, "I'll find you, wherever you are. After the game. Maybe in a day, maybe a week, maybe a month. And I'll make sure you never get another hit again."

My first reaction was pure terror and a chill raced

down my spine. But immediately after that I had another thought. *He'll never be able to find me, because I'll be a girl.* I laughed out loud.

"You think that's funny? he said, obviously startled.

"I do!" I said, and laughed again. "Very funny."

"Well," he sputtered, "you won't think it's so funny when we meet up."

"Oh, no, I'm sure I won't. Now get out of my way. I have a base to steal."

Larry stopped hovering over me and put his glove out for a throw from the pitcher. I looked at Coach Kobrinsky to see if I should steal. Sure enough, he put the steal sign on. Or I thought he had. Cap second time, then ear. And ear was steal. I inched off the bag. David was up to bat.

Larry kept talking. "I'm gonna take your arm and crumple it up like it's a pretzel. Then I'll bake it in an oven!"

"Bake it in an oven? Is that what you do when you're at home?" I taunted him. "Do you bake with your mama?"

His face turned so red I thought there was a good chance he might actually pop.

But I had to concentrate on the pitcher's moves. Just as he threw his first pitch, I took off. I slid into second base. The second baseman missed the catcher's throw, and I was in easy. I almost decided to go to third, but the second baseman recovered quickly. I got up, brushed myself off, and grinned at Larry. He shook his fist at me. I thumbed my nose at him.

It was fun being a boy! I could never thumb my nose when I was a girl. Never. It was fun running in pants, too, and not having to worry about being polite. These boys were *certainly* not polite. Of course, I was used to that from playing with boys in pickup games in dirt lots and alleys. And I wasn't so polite then either, even if I did wear a skirt!

Unfortunately, David struck out in three pitches. Two outs. Izzy was up. He winked at me as he went into the batter's box. I got ready to run. Izzy, I could see, was determined to get me home.

Izzy swung on the first pitch. As soon as I heard the sound of the bat hitting the ball, I took off. If the ball were caught I'd be out anyway, I reasoned. But I didn't see the third baseman's foot as it shot out right in front of me as I rounded the bag. I fell face first with a tremendous thud. I scrambled to my feet, and ran as hard and as fast as I could to the plate. The ball was there before me, and the catcher was blocking the plate. Well, this was not time to play like a girl. I gritted my teeth and ran into him with all the force I could muster, expecting a horrible crash. Their catcher was a stocky, solid fellow.

Wham! The breath was knocked out of me—the little I had left after falling at third—and I tumbled over the catcher. He fell over, but hung onto the ball. I was fast but not heavy enough to knock the ball out of his hand. The umpire yelled, "You're out!" I disentangled myself and started toward the bench.

Even though I'd been tagged out, my teammates gave me a round of applause. I got enough friendly punches on my shoulder that it began to hurt, and I brushed the dirt off myself as best I could. Coach Kobrinsky came over. "Which is the better teacher, success or failure?" he asked.

Before I could open my mouth to answer he said, "Think it over." I grabbed my mitt and headed out to the field.

I considered it as I ran toward the outfield. Getting thrown out at the plate was a failure. But all that had been on my mind when I'd been tripped was that I didn't want the Tigers to get away with cheating—that's why I got up and ran for home. And my teammates were happy. *They'd* thought I was tough. But maybe Coach Kobrinsky didn't think so, or he wouldn't have asked me that question. I wondered why he wanted me to think about the question instead of thinking about the game.

I had just taken my spot on the field when the Tigers' center fielder whacked the bat and sent the ball just past Izzy. The batter easily made it safely to first. The Tigers began to make silly growling noises, something I suppose they did when they had a rally on. I thought they sounded ridiculous.

"Ooh, scary!" I called from the outfield.

My teammates picked up my call. "Ooh scary, scary," they screamed, covering their eyes in mock terror.

While watching the Tigers' second baseman walk up to the plate I continued to think about Coach Kobrinsky's question. Had I returned to third after being tripped, there would have been two outs, not three. I'd be at third and Aaron would have had a chance to hit me home. And Izzy would be on first or second.

So was that failure? And if so, what was I to learn from it? You had to make quick decisions in this game. I smiled to myself. Papa always said to me, "Rosie, stop and think." But I liked to decide and do!

Suddenly the second baseman hit a ball over David's head, which easily moved the runner from first to second. I decided I'd better stop thinking about the coach's question and start paying more attention to the game. The Tigers now had runners on first and second, no one out.

Larry was up again, looking ready to make the most of the moment. Abe went out to the mound to talk to our pitcher, Lew. Lew took a deep breath, then threw the ball to Larry. Strike! Our team cheered. Then another strike. More cheers. A ball. Another ball. Larry swung hard at the next pitch, but it caught the end of his bat, resulting in a grounder to Max. In the meantime the runners took off. Max had to throw to first for the sure out. Larry took his time getting off the field, but no one wanted to make him hurry. He glowered all the way back to the bench.

The Tigers' right fielder came up to bat next. He popped up to Max, two away! The third baseman came up next, with two on and two out. Lew walked him. I tried not to shake my head. What could be worse than walking a batter in this situation? *At least throw strikes and make the guy earn his base.* Bases loaded!

Next their shortstop was up. After taking two balls and fouling off a pitch he took two more balls and he was walked. A run scored, the bases still loaded. I felt like shaking Lew. Instead I called out, "C'mon Lew. You can get him out!"

Morley was up next. Lew threw a strike, but Morley hit it straight to center field. Izzy picked it up on a bounce and threw it in, but not before the Tigers had scored a run. Still, the Tigers had the bases loaded. The game was tied, and I wasn't feeling too hopeful.

But then the Tigers' catcher came up to bat and swung at the first pitch, sending it straight to Max, finally giving us our third out. As I ran off the field, I started to sing "Take Me Out to the Ball Game" at the top of my lungs. My teammates joined in, and by the time we were back at the bench our spirits were much improved.

Hannah's voice cut through our chatter. She was behind the bench again. "Let me hear you sing that song again."

"Why" I said, deeping my voice as much as I could.

"Because," she said, "I like it."

I glanced back at her. She looked innocent enough. But why was she here again? Did she suspect me? I shouldn't have drawn attention to myself. Why couldn't I just play the game and keep a low profile?

She smiled. I pulled my cap down, turned my back to her as I looked toward the field, and said, "Coach wouldn't approve."

"Go away," Izzy ordered his sister.

"Fine!" she declared, and flounced off. But as I looked back over my shoulder, she was looking back at me.

Had she discovered me?

Chapter 5

"I think Hannah likes you," Izzy said.

"What?" I sputtered.

"Honestly, I think she likes you," Izzy repeated.

A crush? She had a crush on me? That might be even worse than if she'd discovered my deception. Or worse still, if she discovered who I really was, she'd feel she'd been duped. I looked quickly over my shoulder again. Sure enough, she was waving happily.

I wanted to go over and talk to Papa, but I was afraid if she saw me talking to him, and knew that Abe was his son, she might make the connection. I glanced at Papa. He was busy with his camera. I noticed that he wasn't shooting constantly. He would shoot for a minute, check his equipment, then focus the camera again.

Well, I thought to myself, I *am* supposed to be Abe's cousin, so Papa could well be an uncle. I could go talk to him and it would seem natural.

Aaron, our first baseman, was up to bat. I sauntered over to Papa. Before he had a chance to speak I whispered to him, "I'm Roy, Papa. Call me Roy."

"Yes, Roy," he said with a broad smile. "How's the game?"

"It's fun. Except that the Tigers' first baseman has threatened to break my arm."

Papa looked shocked. "Not if I have anything to do with it, he won't!"

"Papa," I whispered, "don't worry. After the game, how will he find me?"

"What if he doesn't wait until after the game?" Papa said. "He could make it look like an accident on the field."

I hadn't thought of that. Still, he didn't scare me. "Don't worry, Papa," I assured him. "I'll keep well away from him."

"How?" Papa asked. "Even if you hit a home run, you still have to round first base."

"I'm fast, you know that," I reminded him. "He'll have to catch me first."

As we spoke I watched Aaron go to the plate. Papa

stopped talking as he filmed Aaron, who took a strike and two balls, hit a foul, and then got a solid hit right up the middle. He sprinted to first base.

"I'm shooting some of the plays," Papa explained to me. "And everything you and Abe do." He looked at the sky. "I hope it doesn't rain."

I followed his gaze. The sky was clouding over quickly. "Why don't you make a baseball movie?" I asked.

"That's hardly bringing culture to the people," Papa scoffed. "But this is excellent practice for me."

A couple of men from the Chavarim parents' group came over then to investigate Papa's amazing machine and to talk to Papa about it. I noticed some people coming over from the other team too. Everyone was fascinated and wanted a closer look.

Casually I walked back to the bench. Morris was up to bat. He tried to bunt, but instead hit a high pop up. Their catcher easily took care of that, and Morris threw his bat down to the ground in frustration. One out, with a runner still on first.

Now it was Abe's turn. I saw Papa turn the reel on the movie projector as Abe walked into the batter's box. Abe took ball one. Our team cheered him on. Coach Kobrinsky stood near the third-base line sending signs, but none that I recognized. I sat down beside Izzy.

"Can you tell me what those signs mean?" I asked Izzy, feeling worried. "If I have to follow those I'll have no idea what to do."

Izzy laughed. "Those are Coach's make-believe signs. They don't mean anything."

"Really?"

I watched as Abe took ball two. He looked at Coach Kobrinsky. I noticed that the other team was looking at the coach too—even their pitcher. They were all trying to figure out what play was on. Steal? Hit and run?

"So no play is on?" I said.

"Nope! Abe just needs to hit the ball."

"But why is Coach sending those signs?" I asked.

"At least once a game he does this. If he touches his eyebrow first we know the rest are fake signs and we don't pay attention to them. But the other team doesn't know that."

"But why?" I repeated.

"Coach does it to teach us that there is more to life than what we see. Another level of reality. He says that sometimes God works this way. God will give you all sorts of things to look at and keep you busy, such as work, or school, or worries about friends, so that you can't see that life is really simple. When Coach gives all these phony signals, the other team gets caught up in them. He points out afterward that life is always much simpler than it appears. In this case all Abe needs to do is hit. In life all we need to do is pay attention to God and the oneness of the universe."

I was intrigued. Abe took strike one.

"What if we don't know anything about God," I asked. "How can we pay attention?"

Izzy paused for a moment before he replied. "Well, maybe you should ask Coach that."

"But you study," I said, "don't you?"

Izzy nodded.

"So what do *you* think?"

Abe hit a foul. Two balls, two strikes.

"I think Coach is right. We get caught up in all sorts of things that aren't important."

Just then Abe swung the bat hard. The ball flew into left field and dropped in front of the Tigers' fielder. Abe made it easily to first, and Aaron made it to third.

"Like what things?" I asked Izzy as we clapped and cheered. "What things aren't important?"

Izzy shrugged. "I can't explain it as well as Coach. Just . . . well, there's a voice inside. And if you listen to it, somehow you know the right thing to do. It's hard to explain."

"Is the voice God?" I asked.

Again Izzy shrugged. "Maybe it's God's wisdom."

I looked at Izzy with admiration. He seemed very wise. I liked him. I wondered how he could be so different from his sister. But then a thought occurred to me.

"Does your sister study?" I asked.

"No," he scoffed. "She's being allowed to finish school this year, but she won't go to high school. Mama wants her at home to help. Hannah begged to be allowed to stay at school, but—"

"Do you think that's fair?" I interrupted.

Izzy looked at me strangely. "Fair? It's the way it is."

"Not in our home," I said. "My sister wants to be a teacher." Of course, I was thinking of myself.

Izzy shrugged. "The men need to study, the women need to keep the home."

I thought of all the times Mama had ranted and railed against the Orthodox way. "They want women to be ignorant," she'd say. "It's fine for men. No," she'd add, "it isn't. Because the men are keeping women from reaching their potential. And that is bad for the men, as well as the women." It certainly didn't seem right, or fair, to me.

Lew was up to bat. One out, runners on the corners—but I was more interested in my conversation with Izzy. "Don't you think that might make your sister sad? Maybe she wants to study too."

Izzy shrugged again. "There are many things in life that are hard. She'll get used to it."

I can't say I liked Hannah any better at that moment, but I did pity her. I would be able to go to school—even college—if I wanted. Mama expected it of me, in fact. But Hannah would be able to do none of that. And she was the smartest person in class, even among the boys.

Lew struck out in three swings. He was not a very good batter.

Next up was Crazy Joe. "What'ya got Morley, Sorely," he shouted to their pitcher.

"I've got enough to get you out!" Morley shouted back.

"Let's see it, Sorely, Morley. My peepers are waiting!"

Both benches began to cheer and jeer along with the two players.

Morley threw ball one.

"That the best you got?" Crazy Joe taunted. "My mama throws better than that." He dug in to the batter's box. "My *sister* throws better!"

Our team started to chant, "My sister throws better! My sister throws better!"

If they only knew that Abe's sister was actually playing with them!

Morley threw a strike. Joe swung through it. Morley's

eyes narrowed. As soon as he got the ball back, he threw again—another strike.

Joe backed out of the box. "That's nothing!" he yelled. "Nothing!"

The next pitch was high, but Crazy Joe swung at it anyway and missed. The inning was over. Morley spit on the ground before he walked off. Crazy Joe threw the bat down.

Coach Kobrinsky walked over. As Crazy Joe ran back for his mitt, Coach said, "Who lost concentration there? Him or you?"

Crazy Joe grimaced. "Just thought I'd rattle him a bit."

"If a word is worth a penny," Coach Kobrinsky said, "silence is worth two."

He stopped me before I went out into the field. "Have you thought about my question?"

"I've thought," I answered.

"And?"

"I've thought, but . . . well, what teaches you more: success, or failure? Wouldn't success? Papa always says success builds on success. I mean, failure would make you bitter. Or mean."

"It would. Exactly!" Coach agreed. "So think further. How do you avoid that? Think more. But don't forget," he added, "to pay attention to the game!"

"I won't," I promised. I grabbed my mitt and hurried to my position on the field.

Their first batter was a nice-looking boy, but I was shocked when I heard what came out of his mouth. "You low-lifes got some time off from the poorhouse to come play?" he shouted.

It was obvious that our team was poor compared to theirs, but I thought that was a very mean thing to bring up. We were all Jewish, after all. Shouldn't we be one family? And the parents couldn't help but hear. Some of them spoke English. It would make them feel bad, wouldn't it?

The other players on his team hooted and jeered.

Of course, Crazy Joe had begun the name calling, so it seemed to me our team had to take some of the blame for this nasty teasing.

Lew let loose a pitch and the ball hit the batter in the shoulder. The boy dropped his bat, ran out to the mound, and jumped on Lew. Their team poured off the bench to support their player, and our team raced over to support Lew.

I did *not* want to get in the middle of a fight, but I couldn't afford to stand out, either. I wasn't sure what to do. I jogged in slowly, hoping it would all be over before it started. I was lucky. It was. The umpires, parents, and coaches managed to pull the boys apart and stop anything before it really got started. The home plate umpire, a hefty fellow around Papa's age, quickly put himself between the two boys before they managed to throw any punches. I milled around on the outskirts of the crowd pretending to be outraged.

"Peasants!" I heard their pitcher shout at us. "Bunch of pathetic peasants! Get a haircut!" Someone else yelled at Izzy. "You're not in Russia now, greenhorn!" And the others took up the chant. "Greenhorns! Greenhorns!"

This made our team crazy. Everyone started yelling back, "*Goys!* English!" Now we were practically saying that the other boys weren't even real Jews! *"Goyish Golems! Goyish Golems!"*

Suddenly a voice thundered above everyone else's. It was Coach Kobrinsky.

"Shah!" he screamed.

"Quiet!" screamed the Tigers' coach.

I glanced over at Papa. He was furiously working the camera.

The boys began to quiet down, and their loud barbs and jabs shrunk to grumbling amongst themselves.

"The Talmud says, 'All men are responsible for one another,'" Coach Kobrinsky said. "Are you men or boys?" No one answered. "What is the greatest teaching of the Torah?"

"I'll tell you," said the Tigers' coach, a young man of about twenty or so. "It is 'Love your neighbor as yourself.'"

"He's right!" agreed Coach Kobrinsky. "And that's *not* what I'm seeing today."

The boys muttered some more and then slowly made their way back to their positions and to their bench. The parents and children who'd been watching had also gathered around, and now they started arguing.

"You should teach your children some manners," I heard one of the Tigers' fathers shout.

"Manners?" shouted back a black-hatted father from our team. "That's all you care about? You should teach your children about Torah! About being a good Jew."

"You think we don't study?" A man from the other side shouted back. "Just because we don't keep a kosher kitchen, you think we aren't Jews?"

"That's right!" the black hat yelled back. "You aren't! What kind of Jew doesn't follow the mitzvot?"

"I'll tell you what kind. The enlightened kind!" the first man yelled, his face turning red.

Coach Kobrinsky nudged the umpire, who shouted, "Play ball!"

A gust of wind tugged at my cap, and I looked up to see the clouds steadily gathering. The weather seemed to mirror the mood of the game. The angry fathers backed away from each other, still grumbling and shaking their heads, and returned to their seats with the other parents.

The Tigers' left fielder was on first, because the pitch that started this fracas had hit him. Their center fielder was up next. He took three straight balls from Lew and on the fourth pitch hit a solid grounder past Max, so they had runners at first and second, and no outs. Their next batter swung at the first pitch and sent the ball out to left field. Joe ran back as fast as he could, dived, but just missed the ball. By the time he got it back in, the Tigers had scored two runs and had a runner on second. They began to chant, "Tigers! Tigers! Tigers!" And some of them were chanting, "Greenhorns! Greenhorns!"

Why do boys have to fight all the time? I wondered as I stood out in the field. As far as I could see, the Chavarim were no more greenhorns than the Tigers were goyim. And I was a Jew just like any of the Tigers. So was Abe. We weren't from a religious family. We hadn't studied Torah. Did that mean we weren't as good as the others? Mama didn't think so. On the other hand, I had to admit Coach Kobrinsky and Izzy had made me curious. Maybe studying Torah would be interesting. But once they knew I was a girl, who would teach me? I looked curiously over at the German Jews. Maybe they let their girls learn Torah. When the game was over perhaps I'd go ask someone.

Meanwhile, I was beginning to worry about the game. Lew seemed to have lost his focus. Abe went out to talk to him. The next batter was Larry, the guy who'd threatened me. I was really hoping Lew would get him out.

On the first pitch Larry swung through a strike. On the second pitch he hit the ball directly at me. "Let me catch it, let me catch it," I whispered, as I waited for the ball. And I did! I took the ball from my mitt and threw it in to Lew. Larry glared at me and shook his fist. I would have tipped my hat, but I couldn't, so instead I bowed to him. When I saw the look on his face I couldn't help but laugh.

The next batter hit a sharp grounder to David, who dropped it. The runner advanced to third, and the batter made it to first. I knew the next at bat was very important. Could Lew hold the Tigers to their two run lead?

The batter hit the ball directly to third base. Morris caught it on the fly and threw home. Abe caught the ball and tagged out their runner. Double play!

As we ran off the field everyone clapped Morris and Abe on the back and said, *"Mazel tov! Mazel tov!"*

"Not bad for a greenhorn," Abe grinned.

Our team chanted, "Chavarim, Chavarim," as Max headed for the batter's box.

A drop of rain hit my nose.

CHAPTER 6

Max hit the ball hard on the first pitch. Unfortunately, their second baseman made an amazing play: He backed up and caught the ball on the run.

My turn.

I picked up the bat, and walked to the batter's box. We were down two runs. I really wanted to swing for a homer, but I knew that the important thing was to get on base. Still, a homer would be a sure run, and I wouldn't have to stop at first and tarry with Larry. For some reason, nerves I suppose, I began to giggle to myself, thinking of all kinds of silly rhymes for "Larry." I wouldn't want to marry Larry. Larry was certainly a very hairy fellow, but one you couldn't easily carry.

"Strike one!"

The ball had sailed past me straight down the middle of the plate. And it had been a perfect pitch to hit for a home run! I was letting Larry get under my skin, and losing my concentration.

On the next pitch I swung and missed. Another strike. The third pitch I managed to get some wood on and I fouled it off. The next pitch was so far outside I safely took it as a ball. Finally I made contact, but on the end of my bat. I sprinted down to first as the ball rolled to short, and made it just before a very hard tag on my shoulder by Larry.

I immediately took as big a lead as was safe and looked for a sign from Coach Kobrinsky.

He touched his cap twice and then his ear. Steal. *That* was a relief. I didn't want to spend any more time than I needed to at first.

"I'm counting on you not to make it home," Larry said to me.

"What? You want me to hurt my team? Play against them?" I couldn't believe my ears. Only a miserable no-goodnik would do that.

"Think of it as helping yourself," he said, as David walked to the plate.

"You don't scare me," I said.

"Really? Think I scare your cousin?"

David was getting ready for the first pitch, and I was getting ready to steal.

"What does that mean?" I asked.

But just then Morley got set to pitch. As he started his windup I took off, not looking at what was happening. I slid into second and looked up to hear the home plate umpire yell, "Foul ball. Return to first!"

I brushed myself off and got back to first.

"I mean," Larry continued as if nothing had happened, "if you aren't scared for yourself, maybe you should think about your cousin. Want to be responsible for *him* getting hurt?"

"*I* won't be responsible. *You* will!" I objected, hating Larry at that moment.

"No, your choice," Larry said.

I saw David get ready again. I decided to wait on a pitch, so the Tigers wouldn't be too sure about my steal. David hit the ball though, and I took off as soon as I heard the noise. Unfortunately it was a high fly to left field. As soon as I saw the ball had been caught, I headed back to first.

"Come on, Izzy," I yelled, as Izzy came up to bat. "Just move me to second, away from here," I muttered under my breath.

I danced around first, trying to keep as much distance between Larry and me as possible. What should I do? What if he hurt Abe? Abe was my younger brother. I always protected him. I couldn't let Larry hurt him—not even for a run. On the other hand, if I let Larry intimidate me—frighten me off—I might as well give up and go home. What should I do? I glanced over at Papa and wished I could ask him, but he was happily filming my every move. And that made me realize that whatever I did, Papa would be filming it!

Izzy got ready for the first pitch. I took my lead off first. The pitcher threw over to first instead of to the plate and I had to dive back into the bag. Larry tagged me, almost breaking my shoulder blade with the ball.

"Hey!" I screamed in protest.

"Ooh, you sound just like a little girl squealing," Larry snorted.

That wasn't good. I had to be more careful.

I took my lead again. This time the ball went to the plate and I took off, again sliding into second. When I looked up I realized I'd gotten in safely with no throw. What a relief to be away from Larry.

As I brushed the dirt and grass off my pants, the second baseman spoke to me. "We aren't *all* like him," he said.

"Excuse me?"

"My name's Carl," he said.

"Roy," I responded.

"We aren't all like Larry," Carl said. "In fact, he's not the most popular player on our team, that's for sure."

"Well, thanks," I said, so surprised I honestly didn't know what else to say. I took my eye off Morley and missed the pitch, but Izzy didn't manage a hit.

"So, you new around here then?" he asked.

"Yes. My cousin Abe brought me. I'm just visiting from New York."

Carl's eyes grew big. "All the way from New York? Is it very different?"

Izzy took a strike. I saw the umpire hold up two fingers: one on one hand, one on the other. So the other pitch had been a ball. One and one. Two out. I started thinking about stealing third. I looked over to the coach. He was thinking the same thing! The steal sign was on. But should I do it? Or should I stay put, hope Izzy struck out, and then perhaps get out of the inning without making Larry any madder?

"So," Carl pressed, "what's New York like?"

Suddenly the bat made contact. Izzy was off and running. The ball had been hit in between second and first. I ran, but not as fast as I could have. I had to protect Abe, didn't I? Or did I? Not knowing what to do, I didn't really make a decision—I just didn't put my heart in it. I passed third, and as I was in between third and home I heard the outfield umpire yell, "You're out." I looked over in time to see Izzy being tagged out at first. With a small sigh of relief I trotted to the bench to get my glove.

Just after I got there, Coach Kobrinsky walked up to me. "I've seen you run much faster than that," he said, voice low so no one else could hear. "Had you run as fast as you could, you could have crossed home and scored before Izzy was tagged out. Is there anything you want to tell me?"

I shook my head.

"Sometimes it's good to ask for help if you need it."

I shook my head again.

"I think something is troubling you, Roy, and you're going to have to make a decision of some sort. I've noticed Larry has been talking to you a lot."

I glanced up at him. He was sharp.

"When you make a decision about whatever it is," he continued, "with what should you be concerned?"

I shrugged. "How it'll work out, I suppose. You have to think about how your decision will affect things."

Coach Kobrinsky put his hand on my shoulder and looked me in the eye. "Not quite true, Roy," he said. "The only thing you need to think about is what is the right thing to do. There's no way of knowing what the consequences of your actions will be. You might think of one result, but then you get quite a different result. Do you know why?"

I shook my head.

"Because you are not in control of what happens."

Yes I am, I thought. *If I score, Larry will hurt Abe, and it'll be all my fault.*

"But sometimes you must be in control," I said. "Mama tells me to think before I act."

"She's right," he agreed. "That's where free will comes in. There is a moment between your thought of how to react, and your actual action. That is a moment when you should pause and avoid reacting by instinct. Then you make your decision."

"And do you have to decide what's best?" I asked. I was so intent on the conversation that the sounds around me faded away, and all I saw was Coach Kobrinsky.

"No," he said quietly, but forcefully. "You have to do what is *right*. The rest will follow as it will."

"But what if something bad happens?" I asked.

"It might," he agreed. "But that's not up to you."

"Who's it up to?"

"God," he said simply.

I was confused. "God might make something bad happen?"

"All things come from God," he said mysteriously.

"What we call good, what we call bad. As for me, I've learned that often what seems lucky or good at the time can end up with bad results, whereas something that seems bad at the time can end up being a very positive thing." He paused. "Think about it." With that he motioned for me to get on the field.

I was horribly embarrassed to see that both teams were waiting for me. Oddly enough, none of them seemed surprised by my little talk with the coach, or the fact that it delayed the game. Perhaps they were used to this from Coach Kobrinsky. The Tigers' batter was waiting in the batter's box and their team was chanting, "Tigers, Tigers, Tigers." I hadn't even heard them.

As I trotted out to the field, part of me felt ashamed because Coach had caught me. He knew I hadn't run hard, and I might have cost us a run. He knew it and I knew it. And I also knew from the terrible way I felt that according to him I hadn't decided to do the right thing. On the surface it seemed the right thing was to save Abe. But maybe it was to stand up to the bully.

I took my spot in right field and tried to sort it out. I remembered a phrase Mama used often when advising us children: "No decision is a decision." Maybe that applied to what I'd just done. I didn't stop at third and decide not to score. I didn't try my hardest to score. I let something else decide for me: Izzy getting out at first. No one except the coach realized that I could have tried harder.

But I still didn't know what to do next.

The Tigers' shortstop was up to bat. I watched as he took two strikes in a row, then hit two fouls in a row. He hit a weak grounder to David at second base, and was easily thrown out.

Morley walked into the batters' box. Lew threw him a ball straight down the middle, hard as he could, daring him to hit it. And hit it he did. He slammed it toward right field, and I could see it was going to travel well past my position. My only choice was to turn and run as fast as I could, not tracking it for the moment, then stop at the chalk and hope I'd run it down. I sprinted fast as I could and then turned. It was going over my head, but I could jump high. Fast as a bolt of lighting from the sky a thought forked through my mind: *No one would question it if you let it drop behind you.* And in that second I leaped in the air, high as I could, glove extended, and felt something hit my mitt. I knew I could still easily drop the ball, so I closed my mitt as tight as I could. With my glove in the air, I dropped into a knee bend, and rolled over on my side. I looked up, not sure whether the ball was in the webbing or not. It was.

As I got up, Coach's words echoed in my mind. "Do the right thing for the right reason."

I threw the ball to the infield amidst the cheers of my teammates. I looked over at Papa. He was cheering too. I looked at Larry. He was giving me a death glare.

Something else Coach had said rattled around in my brain. "Between reaction and action there's a place where free will is." But in baseball you had to react so fast that you barely had time to think. I tried to remember how I'd just made that plan. Partly by instinct: I turned and ran. But maybe instinct *is* quick thinking. I'd just decided very quickly what I had to do.

The Tigers' catcher was now in the box. I tried to concentrate and not to look at Larry. But the harder I tried, the more I looked at him.

It was all well and good for Coach Kobrinsky to advise me to do the right thing. But what if I'd just put Abe in horrible danger? I felt terrible all over again.

The catcher laid down a surprise bunt and started to run, but Abe scooped up the ball and made a perfect throw to first. Out!

A one-two-three inning! And we were up to bat again. I probably wouldn't come up to bat in this inning, and I could stop worrying about Larry for a moment. But as I hurried off the field I saw Hannah walking toward the bench, waving to me.

Things were going from bad to worse!

CHAPTER 7

Papa saved me from Hannah, for the moment at least. He waved me over, and Abe too.

Aaron was starting the inning again, just as he had in the fourth, so I wasn't due up to bat anytime soon. Abe was to bat third though, so he was in a hurry as he ran over to Papa.

"What is it?" he asked. "I'm up soon."

"It's a little complicated," Papa began, "but I think I'm going to need your help." I listened to Papa, and tried to keep an eye on the field. Aaron had fouled off a ball to take strike one.

"See that fellow at the end of the park?"

I did. He looked familiar. He was standing at the corner

of the street watching the traffic. "That's Mordechai," Abe said.

"Correct," Papa confirmed. "He manages our nickel-odeon at the end of Maxwell Street." Papa looked around nervously. "He helped me bring the cameras here."

"Cameras?" I asked.

Papa lifted a blanket and showed us another camera.

"Strike two!" I heard the umpire call.

"I don't understand, Papa," I said. "Why do you have two cameras?

"That's the crux of the problem," Papa answered. "This camera"—he touched the one he was using—"is an Edison model. But Edison demands that we pay them a sort of users' fee, and they force us to join with their company. Well, I don't want to. I want to make my own films and edit them myself. And I don't see why I should have to pay a fee to Edison just because the company's big and powerful. But ever since I bought the camera they've been hounding me to sign up with them. And they'll sue me if they discover I'm using it when I haven't signed up because they own the patent on the camera."

"Ball two!"

I must have missed ball one. I was trying to follow what Papa was telling us, but he was speaking very fast, looking around as he did. Something was very wrong.

"Mordechai has been watching out for me," he continued. "We think the men from Edison might have followed us here. If they can catch me using the camera illegally, I'll be done for. So I brought this extra camera. If they arrive, I need to hide the Edison and pretend I've been using the other one all along. The other one"—he pointed to the blanket—"is a cheap copy. It really doesn't work well in comparison."

"Papa, I have to get back," Abe said impatiently. I could see he thought this was all very silly. I thought it was exciting and daring. Papa was a sort of outlaw!

"I'll help you," I offered.

"Good girl."

"Strike three!"

Aaron was out and Morris was up to bat.

"Since we got here I've noticed some suspicious characters in an automobile circling the block," Papa said. "The same ones who followed us here, I think. If they suddenly spring a trap and try to catch me, I'll need the camera to be hidden somewhere, but I can't think where.

I looked around. I was used to finding hiding places from playing ring-a-levio back in New York.

There was a large stand of bushes near the spectators from our team. If we stashed the camera there and some people stood around it, maybe we could get away with the whole thing.

"Ball one!"

"I have to get back," Abe repeated.

"What about over there?" I suggested, pointing out the bushes to Papa.

"I'd thought of that too," he said. "But we'll have to tell the parents that are sitting there and see if they'll help."

I looked over and saw Hannah waving and smiling at me. "Leave it to me, Papa," I said. "I think I can sort that out for you."

"Ball two!"

I sauntered back to the bench, slowly enough that Hannah was able to catch up. I was still nervous about talking to her straight on, thinking she'd surely recognize me, but I hoped that since she hadn't discovered me so far, I'd be safe. I pretended I was engrossed in the game as I said, "My uncle has a little problem."

"I know why you look familiar!" she exclaimed, interrupting me.

I froze and my breath caught in my throat.

"Ball three!"

"You look so much like your cousin Rosie!" she declared. "She's in my class."

"Are you friends with her?" I asked, unable to help myself.

"Well," she said slowly, "not exactly."

"Any friend of hers is a friend of mine," I said. "She's stalwart."

Hannah made a noise somewhere between a grunt and a hiss.

"Ball four!" Morris took his base.

"I'll ask her about you as soon as we get home," I continued, now unable to stop. Hannah's discomfort was too delightful!

"Well, I don't know her well. The other girls are very closed about letting a new girl into our group. But I'm working on them," she assured me.

"That's swell. Really stand-up," I said, trying to talk more like a boy and to sound as little like myself as possible.

Abe walked into the batters' box.

"Actually," I said, noting Papa's increasingly nervous posture, "my uncle needs some help."

"I'm always ready to help!" Hannah lied.

Izzy was right. She must *really* like me!

"It's complicated," I said, "but there's a big company that doesn't want him using that camera, and they're wrong," I assured her. "He should be able to use it. He's paid for it and everything."

"So? *Nu?*" she said.

"There are some goons after him," I stated dramatically.

Abe fouled off the first pitch.

"Really?"

"Really. And he may have to hide that camera. I was thinking maybe in those bushes. And if some people stood around, no one would suspect."

Abe sent a grounder just past the third-base bag. He ran hard and suddenly we had runners on first and second.

"I'll go talk to my mama." Hannah promised. "And some of the others that are here."

At this point I saw Papa take the camera from under the blanket and place it on the tripod. He took the other camera, and wrapped it up carefully in the blanket. At the same time I could see Mordechai signaling from the end of the street. Perhaps the men in the automobile were slowing down, or making more passes around the block.

"I think we need to move fast," I said.

Lew was up to bat. As Hannah hurried back to the other spectators, I could see Mordechai running toward Papa. I also saw Lew lay down a bunt. He was tagged out as the ball dribbled close to the plate, but Morris and Abe advanced a base.

Mordechai got to Papa just as I did. I turned to see Hannah waving me over. Papa said to Mordechai, "It's in the blanket." Mordechai picked it up.

"Follow Rosie," Papa said. "Oh, and call her Roy."

I led him over to the bushes, where Hannah was

gathering a small crowd of people. Just then, everything seemed to happen at once.

Crazy Joe was up at the plate. He smashed the first pitch he got. But before I could see the result of that, a car pulled up at the curb and two men leaped out. They raced over to Papa and grabbed the camera.

Suddenly about ten men who were watching on our side and another five or so from the Tigers' side rushed over to see what was happening. I noticed that the women on our side slowly sidled over to the bushes and stood there talking loudly—some of them calling to where Papa was, some of them cheering what was happening in the game.

On the field, I could see Morris heading for home, with Abe right after him. Crazy Joe's hit dropped in shallow center field. The Tigers' fielder threw the ball home, not in time to get Morris, but quick enough that Abe had to retreat to third. Max was up next, with Crazy Joe on first. I'd be up after that, but I was rushing over to Papa to make sure he was all right.

"Are you *meshugge*?" Papa was screaming. "Put down my camera."

The men were examining it closely.

"Where's your Edison?"

"I'm not using it," I heard Papa reply as I got closer.

"Time out!" I heard the umpire yell as he moved

toward the commotion. Everyone wanted to see what was going on with Papa.

"I can't use it without permission," Papa said innocently.

"You fellows get out of here," one of the parents yelled. "We're playing a ball game!"

One of the Tigers' fathers joined in. "We don't need any trouble here. Go away."

Soon all the men from the game were crowding around Papa, and the Edison men were backing away.

One of them, a tall lanky fellow in a suit that hung loosely on him, held up his hand. "Fine. Fine! Just remember. You need to sign up with us before you can use that camera!"

"I remember," Papa said.

The men turned, got back in the car, and slowly chugged away.

Once the car was out of sight, Papa shook the hand of every single man around. Mordechai retrieved the camera from the bushes, and Papa set it up again.

The umpire called "Play ball!" and everyone returned to their places.

Max walked on four pitches. Bases loaded.

I couldn't help but steal a quick glance at Larry, on first. He gave me an evil grin.

"Do the right thing for the right reason," I repeated to myself. I looked at Abe. He was cheering, "Come on Roy! Bring me home!" The others on the team were clapping, too.

I was well aware that I could tie the game with one swing of my bat. But at what cost to me and to Abe?

I took the first pitch. Strike one.

I looked at Larry. He clapped in approval. I grimaced.

The right thing surely was *not* to let him bully me. The next pitch was clearly a ball, so I let it go. The pitch after that looked good—a little low, but in the strike zone. I gritted my teeth and gave it my best swing. A hit! But instead of a solid hit, the ball popped up to the shortstop, who threw to first. Larry tagged me hard as I crossed the bag.

"Good for you," he said. "You know which side your bread is buttered on!"

I didn't answer. *I didn't get on base, even though I tried. I might as well let him think I did it on purpose,* I thought. *Why put Abe in danger if I don't have to?*

I saw the dejected looks on my teammates' faces and realized that even though I had tried, Larry had thrown off my concentration and my swing. He *had* intimidated me.

"Don't worry," Abe said as he met me at the bench. "You tried."

"Not hard enough," I muttered.

"Next time," Abe said.

"Sure, next time." I agreed, grabbing my glove. Coach Kobrinsky was talking to Crazy Joe, so I was able to jog out to the field without more questions. Out of the corner of my eye I noticed Papa waving to me. Crazy Joe was still talking to the coach, so I ran over to Papa.

"Thank you for helping, Rosie," he said with a big smile on his face. He paused for a second. "You see, sometimes it's important to stand up to a bully. They're bigger than me and stronger, but I'm smarter. And I have two smart children."

I smiled despite myself. "Thanks Papa."

"Now go play your best," Papa said. "You might not get another chance like this."

I hurried to my position and waited for their first batter to hit. He wagged his bat and Lew threw the first pitch. The batter hit it hard to center field. Izzy ran after it, picked the ball off the grass, and threw it in, but the hitter was easily in for a double. The Tigers' next batter was their center fielder, and he took four balls straight for a walk. I started to worry. Lew looked like he'd suddenly lost his bearings. The next hitter was Carl, the second baseman. He watched a ball sail by. On the next pitch he slammed the ball over third, which carried over the chalk line. A three run homer! They were now leading eight to four, and popping up was beginning to look like a bigger and bigger disaster. The Tigers chanted, "Carl! Carl! Carl!" He grinned and accepted all the handshakes and pats on the back as he stepped over the plate.

Still no one out. Abe asked for time so he could talk to Lew. Lew listened. Then he got set for the next batter, who happened to be my 'friend' Larry. As I looked at Larry, I began to get angry. He was spoiling what should have been a wonderful afternoon for me! He was making me struggle with all kinds of troubling questions. And to top it off, he was scaring me. As these thoughts raced through my mind, his bat connected, and I saw the ball heading over to my right. I sprinted toward where I thought it would land. As I reached it, though, doubts attacked me. Don't catch it. Abe could get hurt. Catch it. Larry's a bully. But I just kept after the ball and then made a leap and there it was in my glove!

The entire team cheered. Lew signaled to me, doffing his cap. After that, he struck out the right fielder, and the third baseman popped up to Max at second. Just like that, the inning was over. I ran to the bench and got all the slaps and handshakes from my teammates.

"You turned it around, Roy," Lew said. "I was ready to give up! No kidding."

"Let's get those runs back," Abe yelled to his teammates.

Chapter 8

As I sat on the bench Coach Kobrinsky came over and said to everyone, "The one thing you learn in baseball is you cannot control the outcome. Try your best, do the right thing, and accept the results."

We were down by too many runs, and I wasn't sure our team was up to this challenge. I was impressed, though, with the level of play. There had been few errors, bumbled balls, and sloppy plays. Just as I was thinking this, there was a terrific bobble to our advantage. David hit the ball out to short and it should have been an easy play. But their shortstop dropped the ball as he took it out of his glove, and by the time he recovered, David was on first.

A voice behind me made me practically jump out of my skin.

"I've asked my mama if you could come to us for *Shabbas* dinner," Hannah said practically right into my ear. "She said yes, of course."

Izzy had been listening to us. "Really?" He sounded pleased. "That would be terrific," he said. "We could study afterward."

"Izzy," Coach called, "you're up!"

"Silly," Hannah said. "Aren't you paying attention?"

Izzy ran to the batters' box and grabbed the bat.

"So?" Hannah asked me.

I watched as Izzy took strike one. I had no idea what to say. I didn't want to upset Hannah, but obviously I couldn't accept. If I said no, though, she might get angry, even suspicious. If I said yes, she'd be disappointed when I didn't show up. But what did I care if she felt bad, anyway? She'd been horrid to me from the moment I arrived at school and had *never* shown any signs of feeling bad about it!

I desperately hunted for an answer. Finally I said, "Well, I might be back in New York by Friday. I hope my mama will be better soon."

"Oh, I hope so too," Hannah simpered.

Meanwhile Izzy had swung wildly through two more

pitches. He returned to his seat, dejected. Aaron was up to bat.

"If Roy is still here Friday, he'll come to us for dinner," Hannah said.

I had to explain to Izzy. "Well . . ."

"Yes," Izzy said, "we can study."

That was the second time he'd said that. I was curious. "Do you study every night?"

"I study all the time," Izzy said. "What could be better? On *Shabbas* we study after dinner *and* all day Saturday. You can come to shul with us. You can stay over!"

"But I don't know how to study," I said weakly.

"It's never too late to start," Izzy said. "You read Hebrew, no?"

"Uh, no," I admitted.

"No?"

"No. My family isn't religious."

"Never mind. I'll translate for you what we're studying."

Aaron, meanwhile, had taken two balls, and on the third pitch hit a fly ball to center. It was caught. I sighed. Two out. One on.

Morris stepped up to the plate and swung on the first pitch. It dribbled down the third-base line so slowly that no one could reach it on time. Suddenly we had two on, two out, and Abe was up to bat.

Abe moved into position with that look I knew well on his face. He would get a hit if there were any way to do it.

I heard a distant rumble and looked up at the sky. The single raindrop that had appeared a while ago looked like it was about to be joined by many others. The wind blew hot from the south and the clouds were quickly gathering. Abe swung through the first pitch.

"Wait for your pitch," called Izzy.

On the second pitch Abe swung again and sent the ball foul.

"That's all right. You can do it!" yelled the boys.

On the other side they started calling, "Greenhorn! Greenhorn! Greenhorn!"

Abe worked the count until it was full, taking the balls, fouling off the strikes. He would not give up. Finally he earned a walk. Bases loaded, two out. Lew was up to bat.

I saw Abe standing on first, and noticed Larry say something to him. Abe turned to Larry, said something back, and laughed. Larry said something else, and made his fist into a ball and shook it at Abe. Abe put his hands on his hips and looked defiantly up at Larry. Uh-oh.

Just as Lew hit the first pitch and the ball took off into the air, Abe hit Larry right in the stomach!

The home plate umpire yelled, "Time! Time-out!"

The ball sailed over the center fielder's head and

landed behind him. The runners took off, all except Abe—who was now being dangled in the air by Larry.

Papa ran at Larry. The boys on our team stopped running the bases and ran to help Abe. Our bench emptied. The Tigers' bench emptied. I sprinted to first as fast as I could, but Papa got to Abe and Larry first. He was a good few inches shorter than Larry and much thinner, but he grabbed Larry's arms and pulled so he'd let go of Abe. Larry wouldn't let go, though. As I got closer I could hear Larry yelling, "Take that back! Take that back!"

"Never!" Abe shouted. "I'll never take it back!"

"Get off him! Get off him!" Papa's voice boomed.

"Take it back!" Larry kept shouting. He looked like he might kill Abe, but Abe didn't look afraid.

Soon the other men had joined Papa. Within moments they were able to pry Larry off of Abe.

"Are you all right?" I asked my brother as he walked away from Larry. The men were still holding the bully.

"I'm fine," Abe said, trying to smile.

"What happened?" Everyone from our team was around Abe.

"He said something to me, and I said something back," Abe said.

"What?" I asked.

"I can't repeat it," Abe said. "But he said he was going to hurt me and my cousin."

So there it was. Out in the open. Just like that.

"And what did you say?" I asked.

Abe laughed. "I can't repeat that, either."

The boys slapped him on the back and he grinned.

Larry could still hurt Abe—sometime later, when Papa and his teammates weren't there to help. Larry could snap Abe like a twig.

The umpires were discussing the situation with the coaches. We all crowded around so we could hear what they'd decide.

"You called time-out," the Tigers' coach said to the umpires. "The batting needs to start over."

Coach Kobrinsky, to my surprise, agreed.

"Yes," he said, "I heard the time-out too."

Our team groaned.

"'The first question at the Last Judgment will be: Did you deal honestly with your fellow man?' We all heard the umpire, didn't we?" Coach Kobrinsky asked.

The boys moaned a collective, "Yes."

"And so we know the hit didn't count, don't we?"

"But it was a good hit," Max objected.

"It was. A good hit at a bad time," Coach Kobrinsky said. "Come on. Let's get back to the game."

"What about Larry?" the umpire said to their coach. "Do you have someone you can play instead of him?"

"Actually," Coach Kobrinsky said, "I don't think that'll be necessary. After all, then Abe would have to sit out too, since he threw the first punch. And if that happens, we don't have a team."

"And we don't have any extra players, either," the Tigers' coach agreed.

"Then let's play ball," the home plate umpire said.

As the parents returned to the sidelines Lew took his place at the plate. Abe went back to first, with Larry glaring at him. Papa stood close by, not yet returning to his camera. We all went back to our bench.

The pitcher threw. Lew swung. He hit the ball again, but this time it was a lazy fly ball. Their left fielder had plenty of time to settle under it. As the ball dropped into his glove he held up his arm triumphantly. The Tigers raced off the field chanting, "Tigers, Tigers, Tigers!"

We grabbed our gloves, but if the rest of the Chavarim felt anything like me, they were discouraged to say the least. Eight to four. Not a good score in the seventh inning.

"Roy," Hannah called. "Are you all right?"

I pretended I didn't hear her and grabbed my glove. But the coach had a word for me first.

"Roy," he called. "Over here." He stood on the far side

of the bench. "You can catch more flies with honey than with vinegar," he said.

I smiled. "Papa always says that."

"Go on," Coach said, and I ran out to the field. But what did he mean? Who was I supposed to catch? Did he mean Larry?

Honestly, why couldn't he be a normal kind of coach? Of course, I'd never had a real coach. I'd only played baseball with my brother and his friends on the streets in sand lots. But I imagined that most coaches plotted strategy, urged on their players, and helped them be better at their sport rather than teaching them about life and what it means.

As I waited for Lew to throw the first pitch I started wondering if there was a way to *think* my way out of this mess with Larry. I hadn't honestly considered any solutions other than giving in to Larry or standing up to him. Was there a third way?

Lew threw his first pitch. It was hit by their shortstop on his first swing, right up the middle, and he reached first safely. Lew threw a ball, then a strike to their next batter, Morley, the pitcher. On the third pitch Abe simply missed the ball and it went all the way to the bench. Their base runner advanced easily to second.

I hoped Abe wasn't losing his concentration. It

wouldn't have surprised me if he was a little rattled by that fight. And maybe even a little sore. I looked over at Papa, who was busily filming away. Despite the brouhaha he seemed to be in fine fettle, enjoying himself thoroughly. And I supposed he was happy to be there to help Abe out when he needed him. It wasn't often Papa had time to see us do anything but work; in fact, this was the first time in a long while he'd spent with us outside of the nickelodeon.

I seemed to be losing my concentration too. Morley had three balls and a strike on him. He popped up the next pitch, and Morris caught the ball near third. And then promptly dropped it! I guess Abe wasn't the only one rattled by the fight. And now Morley was on first because of the error.

The Tigers kept chanting from their bench. This time they were shouting, "Drop it! Drop it! Drop it!" Encouraging the rest of us to follow Morris' example, I supposed.

Now the Tigers began chanting their catcher's name. "Steven! Steven!"

They had two on, no one out, and they already had a four run lead. Steven took strike one. On the second pitch he hit a ground ball, and it headed straight for Aaron at first base. Their runners took off, and it looked like Aaron wouldn't make the play; he stumbled on his way to pick up the ball. Steven, seeing Aaron stumble, started to laugh. I could see it clearly from where I was positioned. But then Steven must have momentarily lost *his* concentration because he tripped on his own feet and sprawled onto the grass. He quickly scrambled up and raced to first base. By then Aaron had recovered, and he easily tagged him out.

That gave our team a boost. At least we had one out. Still, the other team had runners on second and third. Barney, their left fielder, was up. He took three balls, and on the fourth pitch he hit a solid grounder to short. Max had to decide whether to try to get the runner at the plate or go to first. The decision was made for him, though, because the runner at third took off at the crack of the bat and was almost home. Max threw to Aaron at first and we got the second out. But they scored a run. Nine to four. And the inning wasn't over yet. I sighed.

The center fielder was up to bat. He swung through the first pitch. Our team cheered. He swung through the second pitch. Even louder cheers. On the third pitch he hit the ball hard to the outfield between center and left. Both Izzy and Joe took off after it. I could see they were both tracking the ball, both determined to get it. It looked like Joe might get there first, but Izzy was surprisingly fast.

They were barreling toward the same point and I suddenly began to worry that they would crash into each other. "Watch it! Watch out," I screamed. But they weren't listening to me. They were both looking up and had their gloves in the air, and I could see them heading straight for each other. Joe was screaming, "I've got it! I've got it!" and then there was a horrible impact as the two boys crashed headlong into each other. They tumbled on the field and rolled over and over on the ground. The other team scored again, and Larry, on the bench, pointed out to the field and laughed. Laughed!

But then Joe was holding up his glove and showing the umpire the ball. He had the ball! Our team erupted in cheers.

The umpire yelled, *"He's out! He's out!"*

Everyone raced onto the field to see if the boys were all right and to congratulate Joe. Izzy sat on the grass, looking stunned. He'd had the wind knocked out of him. But as he gingerly tested his arms and legs, it looked like everything was working. Joe had a huge welt on his cheek where Izzy must have caught him with a hand or leg or something, but it was clear from that big grin on his face that he felt no pain at that moment. Only pride.

Suddenly Joe started to chant, "Greenhorn! Greenhorn!"

We all laughed and chanted along with him. The Tigers then started to chant, "Nine to four, nine to four, nine to four!"

We heard them all right, but we ignored them. Still, if the others felt anything like me, we were mad. We'd had just about enough of them.

Nine to four? Well, the game wasn't over yet!

Chapter 9

Crazy Joe went up to the plate looking a little shaken but determined. I heard him mutter, "Greenhorn. I'll show them. Each of them is nothing but a *bulvon.*" He said it louder. *"Bulvon!"*

We all knew he was calling them blockheads. Some of them knew it too, but from their expressions it was obvious that many didn't understand Yiddish.

"Can't speak English?" Morley answered back.

Crazy Joe slammed the first pitch past Larry and past their right fielder. He ran full speed all the way to third base, where he was forced to hold as the ball came in to the plate. We cheered Joe, and then went on to cheer for Max.

"Come on, Max. One run at a time! Bring him home!"

Max was far more cautious than Joe. He took the first two pitches, one for a strike, one for a ball. On the third pitch he fouled it off all the way to the spectators on our side. Hannah brought the ball back and managed to stop and give me a few words of encouragement. "You'll show them," she said to me. "You and my brother will make chopped herring out of them!"

I couldn't believe how nice she could be when she tried. It puzzled me even more that she had been so downright mean to the real me.

I turned my attention back to Max as the ball was returned to the pitcher. Morley got set and threw again and I could see he put some extra strength into it. Max connected and hit the ball right to second base. I could see Carl make a quick decision. He turned and fired the ball to Larry at first, for the sure out, letting Joe score. With a five run lead, he had made the right choice. But we all leaped up and met Joe as he charged over the plate. Nine to five.

Now it was my turn. Down four runs, I needed to get on base. And I had a plan. I went up to the plate, swung hard at the first pitch and missed it on purpose. When the Tigers' outfield saw me do that, they all backed up a bit, because they knew I could hit and they figured I'd be going for a homer. The next pitch was too high so I let it go. But the following pitch came in low. Perfect. I tapped the ball with my bat and it fell dead just in front of me. I dropped the bat and ran as fast as I could to first, sliding in headfirst. Larry had to leap off the bag to get the ball. He swiped at me and missed. I was in!

"You don't care about your cousin or yourself, I can see that," Larry snarled.

"But I do." I looked over at Papa, and he waved and kept filming. Suddenly I had a tiny slip of an idea. What had Coach Kobrinsky said? "You can catch more flies with honey than vinegar"?

"That's my uncle," I said to Larry.

"So?" he grunted. He threw the ball back to Morley and David came up to bat.

"He's making a film," I said.

Larry actually seemed to show a little interest. "That's a real camera he has. I've never seen one before."

I couldn't believe it. Larry had said two sentences in a row. And neither of them had contained a threat!

"You could be a movie star," I said, talking to him as I kept close watch on the pitcher and David.

"What do you mean?"

Morley called his catcher to the mound for a conference.

"Well, if he likes what he's filmed, he'll show the film in his nickelodeons."

"Truly?"

"Truly." I paused. "But not if anything should happen to me or to Abe. He'd probably look back on this day as a day of evil, and he'd rip up the film and never want to see it again."

"So he'll show this in his theaters?" Larry asked.

"Could be," I replied.

Morley got set to pitch. I inched off the base.

David fouled off the first pitch. I wondered if I'd just got myself into more trouble with this lie to Larry. How was I going to convince Papa to show the film? And was lying better than giving in to the bully? But maybe I could convince Papa to show the film so it wouldn't be a lie.

I looked over at Coach Kobrinsky and saw him touch his cap twice and give the sign for the hit and run. I looked at David and saw him get set. As soon as the ball left the pitcher's hand I ran. I heard the bat hit the ball, but didn't want to slow down. As I slid into second, I looked up. David's ball was dropping just in front of the right fielder. I scrambled up and decided I could make it to third. I ran as fast as I could and got to third standing up, with David just behind me at second.

Now Izzy was up. I could hear Hannah cheering him

on. I looked at Coach Kobrinsky for a sign. He was signaling for me to steal. Steal? He wanted me to steal *home*? Well, Izzy was a good hitter. They'd never suspect. My heart started to thump, and I broke out into a sweat. Here I was, about to try to execute a squeeze bunt! My favorite play.

Izzy turned his back to me for a second and I saw him hold up one finger. Did he want to take one pitch? I thought that's what he meant. I hoped so, because I had to go just as the ball left the pitcher's hand. I couldn't wait for Izzy to make contact. He swung over one pitch, just as I had. Morley got the ball back and got set once again. So did I. He went into his windup. Every one of my muscles was on alert. He threw. I sprinted. About halfway to the plate I saw Izzy tap the ball. It was rolling toward me and toward third. I barreled into home plate and was there well before the third baseman reached the ball.

"Throw to first," the Tigers yelled to the first basemen. He did, but Izzy was there before the throw. Then the ball went wide, and Larry missed it! David kept running from second, and he scored. Nine to seven! And when Larry missed the throw, Izzy took off and sprinted for second.

Aaron was up to bat and Morley was starting to look rattled. The Tigers' coach went out to talk to him, then waved over their third baseman. He trotted over and took the ball as Morley went to third.

The new pitcher threw a couple of practice pitches. Then the umpire motioned for Aaron to step into the batter's box. He took ball one. Then ball two. Then ball three. Our team began to cheer him on. Ball four. We had runners at first and second, one out. Our third baseman, Morris, was up.

He took ball one. This new pitcher was not very good. Then strike one. Then strike two, on a foul ball. Ball two.

A few raindrops fell on my face, and I heard thunder roll far off. I ignored it.

Ball three. All of our spectators were cheering, but I was holding my breath. Morris waited, then fouled off the next pitch. Their pitcher threw again and this time Morris hit it straight down the third-base line. Morley, who had just taken over at third, dived for the ball, but missed it. Izzy rounded third and scored easily. Aaron got all the way to third before the ball was thrown back in. Nine to eight! And still only one out.

Abe was up next. He swung at the first pitch and sent a fly ball straight to center field. Aaron scored. Abe was out, but the game was tied! Nine to nine. The team jumped all over Abe and Aaron as they came back to the bench.

Now Lew was up, with Morris on first. He took strike

one. Ball one. Strike two. We all called encouragement to him. "Come on, Lew! You can do it!"

But suddenly the umpire was calling strike three.

Coach Kobrinsky went over to Lew. I overheard him say, "Don't carry that bat with you onto the field. Concentrate on your pitching. If you can hold them, we can score in the ninth."

Lew nodded and walked out to the mound. I grabbed my glove and ran out to the field. The wind had picked up, and a light rain had begun to fall. I could barely feel it, though, I was so excited. We could beat them. I knew we could!

Carl stepped up to the plate. Lew got set. He threw. And Carl hit. The ball, high and long, was heading toward center right field. I ran. Izzy ran. But I already knew I wasn't going to get it. I ran as fast as I knew how, only to see the ball drop well over the chalk line. I stopped at the line, bent over, and tried to catch my breath. Ten to nine.

I heard Izzy curse. I didn't think Orthodox boys were allowed to curse. I supposed he'd have to apologize to God later.

We both went back to our places. The Tigers' bench had erupted in cheers; their spectators were clapping and shouting.

As the noise died down I heard Coach Kobrinsky call, "'Act while you can: while you have the chance, the means, and the strength.'"

He truly was the oddest coach who said the oddest things. But I had to admit that he was right. We still had a chance to act. The game wasn't over. It would be, though, soon enough.

I took my position and vowed to try as hard as I could for as long as the game was on. As Coach said, the outcome might not be up to me, but the effort I put in was.

I glanced at Papa, who was clapping, calling to us not to give up. His assistant, Mordechai, was holding the blanket over the camera as a cover.

Lew threw his first pitch to Larry. He took it: ball one. On the second pitch, Larry hit the ball hard toward David at second, who made an easy throw to get him out at first. I was then thankful he hadn't hit the ball anywhere near me. But he still glared at me before he headed back to the bench.

Next their right fielder was up. On the first pitch he bunted. It dribbled just slightly over to third, and then Abe made an amazing play, diving for the ball and throwing to first from his knees to get the runner in time. Two outs.

Pete, the new pitcher, was up next. Lew threw him a strike. Then a ball, then another ball. One more strike. Two and two. On the next pitch he got a hit: a short fly ball to left field. My heart sank. It was too far in for Joe, too far out for Morris. But just as I thought it would drop in for sure, Joe came from nowhere, slid, and caught the ball. The inning was over, but they were still one run ahead. And I knew that at the bottom of the ninth they'd be starting with the heart of their order. *If* there was a bottom of the ninth. First we had to at least tie it up. The good news? The top of our order was up to bat—Crazy Joe.

Chapter 10

So Crazy Joe was starting the inning again, and I would surely get a chance at bat as well. I looked at Larry on first and wondered what he'd decided. Would he go for my bribe?

As if reading my mind, Coach Kobrinsky came over, stood behind Izzy and me as we sat on the bench, and spoke.

"Don't worry about tomorrow. Who knows what may happen to you today?" And then he moved on to speak to some of the other players.

Coach did make a good point. Larry could trip and break his own leg tomorrow. Being in a movie by Papa might tempt him to be nice. If he was going to hurt Abe or me, well, I guessed I'd have to deal with that when and if it happened. Right now, though, there was a baseball game to win. I smiled inside, thinking that so far I'd fooled everyone into thinking I was a boy. No one had even suspected, probably because they'd never think a girl could play baseball better than most of them.

The Tigers were chanting, "Pete! Pete! Pete!" to encourage their pitcher.

Joe swung at the first pitch then yelled at Pete in Yiddish, "You pitch like a girl!"

I giggled. But then I thought, *Boys don't giggle! Trouble!* Nervously I glanced sideways at Izzy. He was laughing at what Joe had said and hadn't noticed my mistake.

The Tigers changed their chant to "Greenhorn! Greenhorn!"

Joe gritted his teeth. We were all sick of that particular insult. Joe swung through the next pitch. Strike two. He fouled off the third pitch. On the fourth pitch he connected, and the ball carried into the outfield. We held our breath until their center fielder tracked the ball down and hauled it in.

One down. Max was up to bat next. He took ball one. He swung through the next pitch. Strike one. On the following pitch he hit a line drive to third base. Morley bobbled the ball slightly and threw to first, but too late to catch the speedy Max.

My turn. I took a deep breath. I *needed* to get a hit. Get on base. *Anything* to keep the inning going. This pitcher, Pete, was not as good as Morley. I'd noticed that he often let pitches go right over the middle of the plate. I just needed to focus, keep my eye on the ball, make contact, and leave the rest up to fate, the way Coach Kobrinsky said.

I swung the bat around, then stepped into the batter's box. As the first pitch came at me, I gritted my teeth, put all the strength I had into it, and swung hard. *Thwack!* Max ran. I ran. The ball kept going. I heard my teammates shout. I even heard Papa shout; and as I ran, out of the corner of my eye I noticed the camera trained on me. The ball kept going. And going.

Finally the ball came down. The outfielders didn't try to catch it. I was rounding second and heading to third when I heard, "Home run! Home run!" I slowed down and looked. The center fielder was running past the chalk to retrieve the ball. Max crossed the plate to tie the game.

The entire team was waiting for me as I crossed the plate. Eleven to ten. We were in the lead. We could win! My teammates mobbed me, sending me to the ground, everyone jumping on me, screaming, laughing, rubbing my head, patting my back, hugging each other and me. Finally the umpire yelled, "Play ball!" Play ball!" and everyone got off me.

I scrambled up from the ground, a grin as wide as a river on my face, I'm sure. But instead of running back to their benches, everyone froze, jaws open, eyes wide, speechless.

"What?" I said, looking at Abe for an answer.

He pointed to my head.

I put my hand up to my head and felt hair. I looked down and saw my hat on the ground. My hair was pinned up in a tight braid, but without the cap, everyone could see I was a girl.

Coach Kobrinsky pushed through the circle. For once even *he* was speechless. The other team's coach pushed through too, saying, "What's going on?" He stopped dead when he saw me. And then he began to laugh. Hard.

"Well, well, well," he said. "Isn't this an interesting development?" He turned to the umpire at home plate.

"What do you propose to do about it?"

Coach Kobrinsky spoke. "I assure you," he said, "I had no idea!" He looked at Abe. "Who is this, really?"

Abe kicked the dirt. Looking down, he answered, "My sister."

Slowly the other team was coming off the field and crowding around us. I was embarrassed and humiliated at being caught. On top of that I felt bad, as if I'd let down my new friends, and my coach.

Suddenly a shriek cut through the air. Hannah pushed a couple of the boys aside. "You! It's you!" Then without warning she leaped at me and smacked me hard with an open hand across one cheek.

Well, no one hits me, especially not Hannah! I flung myself at her, grabbed her hand, and wrestled her to the ground. Everyone started shouting. Then I heard Papa's voice boom over everyone else's. "What on Earth is going on?"

I felt his hands pulling me off Hannah, and I saw her brother Izzy pull her away from me. "You're a monster," she screamed at me. "A monster!"

Everyone started talking and shouting at once—the players from the Tigers, their parents, the players from the Chavarim, their parents. I couldn't hear anything. Papa held on to me, his arm firmly around my shoulder as if to protect me. Finally he spoke.

"Shah! Shah!"

Slowly everyone quieted down.

"I don't see what all the fuss is about," he said, when it was quiet enough for him to be heard. "My daughter was asked by her brother to step in for an injured player. It's true she isn't a boy, and she did deceive you, and that's not good. But she wouldn't have been allowed to play because of your silly rule about girls. Morally, my wife and I believe that rule to be wrong. We believe girls should be treated as equals. We are free thinkers!" he declared proudly. "Sometimes you have to break a rule if the rule is wrong. Rosie behaved well. She played well. And she may have just won the game."

"That's true," the Tigers' coach said. "So all her runs should be disallowed! We've been deceived. This entire game shouldn't stand."

"Maybe that should be left up to the umpires," Papa said. "Isn't that why they are here?"

The other umpire had come in from the outfield. The two looked at each other and the home plate umpire said, "Well, this is a new one for me, that's for sure. Still, we'll have to make a ruling. We've heard from the Tigers. What does the coach from the Chavarim have to say?"

Coach Kobrinsky gazed at me thoughtfully and then at the umpires. "Rabbi Nachman of Bratslav would say, 'Rather a man die than lie.'"

I was shocked. That seemed rather severe. Especially since I was used to telling white lies. Last year I pretended to be sixteen so I could work instead of Mama. This time I pretended to be a boy so I could help Abe win a baseball game. Death? That hardly seemed a punishment to fit the crime. I felt my eyes fill with tears. It hurt to see the coach turn on me.

"Of course," he continued, "an exception casts light on a rule. Abe's father has a point, that sometimes rules need to be broken."

"How can you say that?" one of the fathers, dressed in a black hat, said. "She's a female! Why, my son has been dirtied, playing on the same team. It is forbidden! The Torah tells us to stay far away from falsehood."

"And yet our patriarch, Aaron," Coach Kobrinsky said, "told white lies in order to bring peace. This," he continued, "is not a case of peace, but a case of winning at all costs. Surely deception is not acceptable under those circumstances." He paused. "What do you say . . . what is your name?"

"My name is Rosie," I answered, straightening my shoulders. I wouldn't be cowed by anyone.

"Rosie," Joe interjected, "I think you're a great player!"

I almost smiled.

"So do I!" Abe said.

"This was all your idea, I suppose," Coach Kobrinsky said, looking at Abe.

"Yes," Abe admitted.

"I think they should forfeit and that should be the end of it," the Tigers' coach interrupted.

"But," Coach Kobrinsky said, "is it fair to punish the entire team because of one"—he looked at Abe, then me—"or two people?"

Everyone started arguing again. I saw the umpires talking to each other. Papa squeezed my shoulder, and Abe came to stand beside me.

"Never mind, Rosie," he said. "You played great."

I did, I thought. *I played as well as any of those boys!* I looked up at Papa. He gave me a wink. Maybe this was a lesson he didn't mind me learning. He must have known I might be found out. I wondered if that was one of the reasons he had made sure he'd be there—to help me if I needed it. What a good papa he was!

"Hold your head up," he whispered into my ear. "Hold your head up and take responsibility."

I nodded.

"I'd like to say something," I said. No one heard me.

Papa spoke, his deep voice rising over the din. "Please listen. Rosie has something to say."

"I'm sorry," I began, "for tricking you. But I wanted a chance to play—a chance girls never ever get. And that isn't fair, is it? That girls can't play? Because you can see I'm as good as any of you."

"Better!" Abe interjected.

"I'm sorry you've been tricked. And whatever you decide, I'll respect it. But I don't think we should forfeit the game, because no one on my team knew who I am, and they shouldn't be punished." I stopped.

Papa gave my shoulder another squeeze. "Good girl," he said.

The umpires walked away from everyone and consulted. In a few moments they returned and the home plate umpire said to the other team's coach, "Would you allow her to play through the rest of the game?"

The coach answered right away, "No. Not so much because she's a girl, but because she was here under false pretenses."

The umpire looked at Coach Kobrinsky.

"No," he agreed. "First because she's a girl, and my team cannot accept that. Second, because she deceived us."

That was why Mama was so against religion. Why did they insist on treating girls so differently? I felt mad at Coach Kobrinsky. He had seemed so wise. But this wasn't wise, was it? And none of my teammates stuck up for me.

The umpires walked away again to discuss the situation. Parents from both teams shouted at each other back and forth. Finally the home plate umpire returned and held up his hand. Slowly the parents quieted down, and the umpire spoke.

"The game will continue. The score will stand. But Rosie will not be allowed to continue to play. The Chavarim must play the bottom of the ninth with no right fielder—and Rosie will not be able to bat again. If there is any further disagreement," he continued, "you can always appeal our decision after the game." He looked up at the sky. A light drizzle was falling, the wind was up, and the thunder was getting closer. "I suggest we continue now," he added, "or we'll be rained out."

The parents returned to their spots, and the coaches shooed their players back to the field. I didn't know what to do or where to go.

"You come with me, Rosie," Papa said. "You'll be able to see fine from where I'm filming."

I took Papa's hand and followed him, thankful he was there and glad to be away from both teams. Izzy was glaring at me worse than the members of the Tigers. I shook my head, thinking about school on Monday and how Hannah would torture me even worse than before.

As we got back to the camera, Mordechai was practically jumping up and down. "I shot all of it," he exclaimed. "You running over," he said to Papa, "and Rosie with her hat off! It's going to make quite a story."

Larry was back at first. He looked at me in a rather puzzled way and then motioned me over. Reluctantly, I hurried over, as they hadn't started play yet.

"Was this all part of the film?" he asked.

"What?"

"Was this all part of the story?"

"Oh!" I saw what he was saying. But remembering what Coach Kobrinsky had said, I hesitated to lie. On the other hand, if it would save Abe and me . . .

"You don't have to say anything," Larry winked at me. Then he paused. "You play good for a girl."

"Thanks," I said, shocked.

"I must have scared you," he said. "I don't like to scare girls. I'm sorry."

Suddenly being a girl was going to help me? It was all so confusing. I felt like telling him he should feel free to scare me just like he would any boy, but that wouldn't make any sense.

"Play ball!" the umpire called. I rushed back to Papa and crossed my fingers. David was up next. On the third pitch he hit a ball to their shortstop. He threw to first, but Larry dropped the ball just as David crossed the plate. We had a player at first.

Somehow I still wanted to win—still thought of the Chavarim as my team. Even if they had rejected me, they couldn't take away the game I'd played. I had been part of the team.

"It's still Abe's team." Papa said, "Cheer for him."

The only thing was, I wasn't sure I liked Abe's team anymore.

Izzy was up to bat. He hit the first ball right to short.

The shortstop threw to second, the second baseman threw to first, and just like that the top of the inning was over.

Their team ran off the field and ours ran on. Right field was empty, of course, so Joe played left center, Izzy right center.

The Tigers' batter took the bat in hand and stepped into the box. Morley began their teams' chant: "Beat the girls! Beat the girls!"

I got more nasty stares from my old teammates. And I started to get angry. Without me, they wouldn't be winning right now. Why had none of them stood up for me except Joe? What was the matter with them?

"I suppose no one likes to be tricked," I said out loud.

"That's true Rosie," Papa agreed. "You can't expect them to like that. You wouldn't."

The first batter, the shortstop, struck out. Morley moved into the box. He swung at the first pitch and sent it sky-high right behind home plate. Abe screamed, "I got it. I got it!" And he did get it! Two out.

Their catcher was up.

He took ball one. Ball two. Ball three. His team was cheering. He took the next pitch, but the umpire called it a strike. He fouled back the next one. But finally he hit a ball to right field. It would have been an easy play for me, but Izzy couldn't reach it and it dropped in for a double. Their team erupted in cheers. With just one more hit they could tie the game.

Their left fielder was up next. He swung at the first pitch and missed. He swung at the next pitch and hit the ball to third. Morris grabbed it, ran to the base and managed to tag out the runner coming from second.

That was it. We won!

Our team erupted in cheers. They jumped all over each other celebrating.

But I turned away. I felt horribly left out. A pat on my back made me turn. It was Abe.

"Thanks, Rosie!" he said. "You were great."

To my surprise Joe was right behind him.

"Rosie," he said, "you helped us win."

Behind him was Aaron. "Good game," he said, and held out his hand. I shook it. Behind him was Lew. "Good game," he grinned. And then David. "Good game," he said.

"Thanks. Good game," I replied.

Max, Izzy, and Morris were not with the others. They stood back, purposefully ignoring me. Still, my heart lifted, and I felt happy again.

Coach Kobrinsky walked over to Papa and me.

"May I say a word to Rosie?" he asked Papa.

Papa looked at me. I nodded.

Coach Kobrinsky motioned me away from the others. We walked a short distance.

"In the days ahead, Rosie, think back on this afternoon," he said. "You'll see that this game is very much like your life. It begins, it must end, and everything in between is a tapestry of your choices, others' choices, and fate. Think back over the game and you'll see what I mean."

"Aren't you mad at me?" I asked.

"Why should I be?" he asked.

"Because I tricked you."

He smiled. "You're young, Rosie, you are still learning. And I'm older. And *I'm* still learning. What you have to think about is what your intention was. Was it to trick me? Was it to prove something? Or maybe was it to help your brother?"

I thought. "Maybe the last two," I said.

"Well," he answered, "perhaps the last reason would have been a good one. Good enough to lie for, though? Just remember it's up to you whether you learn from events and choices—and even fate—or not. That's the important thing."

"Coach! Coach!" Some of the parents were calling to him—no doubt to complain further about me.

"One more thing, Rosie. Cabala teaches us that events

that *seem* good often end up with results in your life that are not good—and vice versa."

I looked at him, confused. He had said something like that earlier but I still didn't really understand. "How could that be?"

"You'll see," he said. "Good-bye, Rosie."

"Good-bye, Coach Kobrinsky."

Suddenly the skies opened up with full force.

"Rosie, Abe," Papa called. "Come. We must get this camera out of here!"

I turned and ran to help Papa. Everyone on the field began to leave as fast as possible as the rain pelted down.

I couldn't believe it had only been a few hours since we started to play. It felt like a whole lifetime to me.

Chapter 11

It was exactly two months to the day after the game when my life changed drastically—and all because of that game.

I'd spent plenty of time thinking about what Coach Kobrinsky had said. In a way he'd been right. The game had been a revelation of a sort. While I was in the middle of it, all I could concentrate on was Larry and what to do about him. But mixed in with those worries were triumphs. That home run I hit was so special, it was like a star streaking across the sky.

When my cap came off and I was discovered, all I could think about was how embarrassing it was and how everyone hated me. But then Coach Kobrinsky told me that often things weren't what they seemed. And things did turn out so differently from the way I expected they would. For one thing Carl, the Tigers' second baseman, and I became friends. At school Hannah hated me more than ever, but it didn't matter because Carl would meet me after school. We'd play catch or stickball with his friends. He had a sister one year younger than me, and we became friends too! I soon discovered that his family went to shul. They were Reform Jews, and he studied—but more importantly, so did his sister. Who would have thought? Papa agreed that next year I could cut down my hours at the nickelodeon so I could go study after school with them.

But two months later, that's when the truly unexpected burst upon us. Papa came home for dinner Sunday night after a busy day at the nickelodeon. We'd been working there too, naturally, but everything had seemed normal to us. Mama had made us a nice stew for dinner, as it was getting very cold out.

As we were eating Papa said, "I have to tell you children something Mama knows already." He paused. "Here it is. You know that I filmed the game that day Rosie played?"

We all nodded. I had tried to convince Papa to splice it and show it at his theater but he'd refused, even though it was to save Abe from Larry. (When Larry found out I was a girl he'd stopped threatening me, but at first I hadn't been sure if he'd still carry out his threats on Abe. Papa predicted that Larry would lose interest in Abe and me. It turned out that Papa was right. We didn't see or hear from Larry again.)

"Well, somehow, by mistake," Papa continued, "Mordechai sent the reel to New York, to my partner Mr. Jacobson. He thought it was a new picture. He put music to it and began showing it. Well," Papa continued, "it's become the biggest hit on the circuit! And Mr. Jacobson wants me to make another one. But we can't make more movies here, as it's almost winter."

He looked at Mama, and she nodded encouragement. "Go on," she said. "Out with it."

"We're going to move," Papa announced. "To California, where it's warm, and we can make movies all winter."

No one spoke. I was too stunned. I suppose Abe and Joe were too. We'd only been in Chicago less than a year, after all.

"Oh," Papa added, "did I mention, that Rosie turned out to be the star of the movie? Everyone loves her. So she's to be the star of the new one."

"Me?" I asked.

"Yes, Rosie. When your hat came off, Mordechai kept filming. Now the audiences in New York cheer when they see you triumphing in the end."

"But they pulled me from the game," I objected. "I didn't triumph—I was disgraced!"

"Not in the movie. The movie ends with your home run and your cap coming off," Papa told me. "See, that's the difference between real life and the movies. In the movies we can make a happy ending!"

Mama smiled. "And Papa will make movies like no others—movies that uplift, movies that educate. I'm even thinking of helping him."

"Really, Mama?" I asked.

"Really. I enjoyed managing the nickelodeon. I'll never give up on my union work, but I don't want to return to the factory. So. Why not? It will be a wonderful way to educate women."

"Will we like it there?" Joe asked.

"It's summer all year round, and oranges and lemons grow on trees," Papa said. "We'll buy our own home! And we'll make movies."

I thought back to Coach Kobrinsky and how his first words to me were something about how there was more to life than meets the eye. How true that was. Fate was working away the entire time and I hadn't realized it.

"It's *b'shert,*" Mama said, as if reading my mind.

"Yes, it's meant to be," Papa agreed.

"I thought you didn't believe in God," I said to Mama.

"I said I didn't believe in religion," Mama answered. "That's different."

"Well then," Abe said, "I suppose we have to go."

"And besides, I love lemons," I said.

Papa laughed. "Rosie, that's just like you. Other children, they love oranges. You, you love lemons."

I grinned. "Maybe I'll be a famous actress one day!"

"Who knows what fate has in store," said Papa. "California, here we come!"

A Note to My Readers

I love baseball. I came to the game late in life, 1986. I began to watch it with my dad, when he was sick and couldn't concentrate on anything else. I started as a Mets fan but soon became a Blue Jays and Cubs fan. The day the season ends is a sad day for me, and opening day is a thrill. I do believe that baseball is a metaphor for life and lessons are always there for learning.

When Rosie moved to Chicago I immediately thought of the Chicago Cubs and began to research baseball history. I began on the Cubs' Web site, http://chicagocubs.mlb.com, a wonderful site that includes the team's history. I also used www.baseball-almanac.com. I then read *The New Bill James Historical Baseball Abstract,* a wonderful book full of fascinating facts ranging from what the players wore to how they spoke; *The Chicago Cubs,* by Warren Brown; and *The Golden Era Cubs* by Eddie Gold and Art Ahrens.

While researching Jewish history in Chicago, I was lucky enough to find the books *The Jews of Chicago: From Shtetl to Suburb,* and *Jewish Chicago: A Pictorial History,* both by Irwin Cutler. I also found some wonderful Web sites on Chicago, especially www.aviewoncities.com/chicago/chicagohistory.htm.

I'd like to thank my editor, Jen Weiss, for her helpful comments, her understanding of the book, and her enthusiasm; and my agent David Bennett, my friend Morri Mostow, and my husband, Per Brask, for their encouragement. My friend Perry Nodelman was always willing to help me brainstorm. And special thanks to Michael Nathanson, who helped me settle on the structure of the book and read it for any baseball errors. If there are mistakes the fault is mine, not his.

I hope my readers will feel the wonder of the game as I do and that they will follow Rosie on to Los Angeles and another adventure!

Yours,
Carol Matas